T0290336

VOLUPTUOUS PLEASURE

Voluptuous Pleasure

THE TRUTH ABOUT THE WRITING LIFE

Marianne Apostolides

BOOKTHUG 2012

FIRST EDITION

copyright © Marianne Apostolides, 2012

The production of this book was made possible through the generous assistance of the Canada Council for the Arts and the Ontario Arts Council.

LIBRARY AND ARCHIVES CANADA
CATALOGUING IN PUBLICATION

Apostolides, Marianne
    Voluptuous pleasure : the truth about the
writing life / Marianne Apostolides.

(Department of narrative studies ; no. 6)
ISBN 978-1-927040-03-4

    1. Apostolides, Marianne. 2. Authors, Canadian
(English)--21st century--Biography. I. Title.
II. Series: Department of narrative studies ; no. 6.

PS8601.P58Z53 2012   C813'.6   C2012-900303-4

PRINTED IN CANADA

For Simi Rowen

It is the misfortune (but also perhaps the voluptuous pleasure) of language not to be able to authenticate itself. The noeme of language is perhaps this impotence, or, to put it positively: language is, by nature, fictional.

– Roland Barthes, *Camera Lucida*

Table of Contents

The Subject of the Game

The object, my father said, was to keep the ring rolling: to go as fast as you could, tight around each obstacle, tapping the ring with a stick. If the ring toppled or touched a marker, you were automatically eliminated. This was the game, as described to me one afternoon, the tape recorder placed between us.

The memory came when we were discussing shrapnel.

That was a game, too, he said: trading shrapnel after an Allied air raid.

"And at the end of an air raid, you'd run around and find your friends: *'My piece is sharper than yours! Look at this one: This one's worth two of your pieces!'* You know, Marianne, you learned how to live with it. In between, you were a kid again."

In between the bombings, the lack of food, the abduction of his father; in between the Italian invasion and Nazi occupation, the Greek Civil War that pitted Communists against Conservatives; somewhere in those fourteen months when my father waited, hoping his father would soon return home: in the in-between, my father was a kid again.

I wanted to find him.

Tap the ring, control its motion, fast but tight around each curve.

I wanted to lead him there.

"And there was another game, too," he says.

❧

"This kid walked in the house. About midnight, late night, it was curfew time; it was the middle of winter, *cold* as hell, and this little kid – couldn't have been more than three or four years old – knocked at the door. He was in rags. Mom opened the door, let him in. But they didn't want him in the house, because they were afraid of disease. Meningitis, influenza, tuberculosis: these were real concerns. But they brought him in and gave him a chair. And we stayed away from him – they wouldn't let us go anywhere near him. And they gave him a big plate of soup, whatever else they could give him, and he ate. And then they opened the door and let him go. In the middle of the night.... Who knows."

"And what do you feel as you say that?"

"Not happy thoughts. You know, 'That could be me. *Will* it be me? Will this ever end?'"

"Were you scared? Did you want that kid gone? How do you react to a child who –"

"Because you were told, '*Don't* go near him. Don't go near.' It's like you're looking at a wild animal in a zoo; you couldn't touch him, you couldn't talk to him, you couldn't breathe his air. And that's how you looked at him: you were afraid of this person."

"He was a vector."

He was a boy.

My father never examined his past until I started asking

him questions. "I want to know the stories," I said. He complied, tenderly acquiescing because I am his daughter, and he loves me. He didn't know what this process would do to him; he didn't know what I was asking.

I didn't know.

I wanted to story of my father.

He gave it to me and I held it like unformed flesh in my hands.

"But in retrospect," he says, "you think of that; I mean, you think of the suffering. There he is, all by himself: barefoot, skinny, with rags, shaved head because of lice, pitch dark and cold outside.... Did he make it? Who knows."

∽

My father grips the stick, curving around a corner. He isn't the type to go faster than he can control. He's determined, though: determined and disciplined. He will be among the fastest, but only through control – through control and discipline, not through risk.

He speeds along the straightaway. He sees two homes – the homes that abut his backyard, sharing a fence. These are the homes that were overtaken by German soldiers. They'd once been owned by Jewish families; one girl had been in his class.

Tap the ring, turn the corner. Go past the houses where Germans sleep.

These houses were converted into barracks. They were also used as anti-aircraft stations, with a wooden walkway connecting the two rooftops. Here the Nazis placed anti-aircraft guns: four-chambered *ack-acks* aimed at British airplanes. Their fire echoed between the buildings.

"When you're talking about the anti-aircraft fire, with the echo that you mentioned, do you –"

"I can hear it right now," my father says. "It was deafening; it's a deafening sound…. Deafening, deafening, and you don't know where to go. You want to run but you don't know which way to run."

"Because it's everywhere?"

"Echoing everywhere, everywhere. And frightening. And airplane engines and *ack-acks* and you're running to safety – where?… Just running is more like it."

"Do you remember having nightmares?" I ask.

"No. You just reacted. You didn't get up in the middle of the night screaming."

"Did you *ever* scream? When you're hearing this anti-aircraft fire, are you screaming?"

"No, no: you're just running. Your first instinct is to run: you cannot stay where you are. Everybody's running. Everyone around you is running. In the streets, people are running. People are pushing to get into a store or a shelter – to get into some kind of safety. And at the end of the raid, you look out at a totally deserted street. *Totally* deserted: you don't even see a mosquito flying around. And quiet," he whispers. "And eerie."

His voice has been flayed. This movement was too fast – this rush from 1942 to now. Time was ripped through his throat; I can feel my hand inside, grabbing the memories.

He sips some water. "No," he repeats, "you didn't scream."

Touch the ring. Tap the ring. Keep control of this motion.

 су

For fifty years, no one knew his story.

For seven years, I asked him questions, eliciting his memories.

For ten years, I tried to gather those memories into a narrative: a single, cohesive, written account that captured the story of his childhood.

For ten years, I failed.

ℰ↷

Tap the ring: this is the game.

'We know who you are, Taki Apostolides.'

"Early on, it was the sense of: *What is Communism?* What does it mean to different people? There were a lot of words thrown around – proletariat, bourgeoisie, that sort of thing. I remember people standing on the corner and expounding their views until they started getting arrested, or went up to the mountains. They'd go up to the mountains to join the guerrillas."

"Were you scared of them?"

"Oh yeah, yeah. Absolutely. Because you felt the threat to the whole family. When dad was killed, it was like, 'I may very well be next.' Because young people were killed, too. So there was always the concern that you would be a target. So you learned how to hide, how to stay in the shadows, how not to draw attention to yourself. You didn't say your name; if they asked about your family, your father, you avoided it."

"Who's 'they'?"

"Anyone, anyone… and I can see him right now, like he's coming in this door…. The corner store… there was a kiosk and behind the kiosk was another store that sold candy and stuff. That corner belonged to a short guy – he wore a hat just like the hat I'm wearing right now, always wearing an apron – and he sold candy and cigarettes and newspapers, that sort of thing. Well, his son was an avowed Communist. And every opportunity he had, he would talk about it. An anemic-looking young man, you know, with pale skin and a big Adam's apple. A sickly looking kid. But he would *shout it out!*"

'Greece for the people! Freedom for Greece!'

"He would *shout!*"

And then he would whisper: 'We know who you are, Taki Apostolides. We got your father and we can get you, too.'

I can see his larynx, that protrusion of cord sliding along his pale throat.

"We know who you are."

Tap the ring.

This game requires precision: velocity interacting with impact, direction; the force of the tap and the shape of the ground – slopes, bumps – irregularities in the ring itself. To win the game, you need to anticipate potential problems; everywhere, calculating, you need to control what hasn't yet happened.

Tap the ring, faster.

The newsagent's son was killed during Round Three of the Greek Civil War. Agamemnon Apostolides was killed during Round One. During Round Two, the adversaries – Communists versus Conservatives – fought in the streets of Athens. Although the Communists were badly defeated, they nonetheless killed 5000 Conservative civilians, dumping their bodies in mass graves; they then captured 10,000 soldiers, forcing them to march barefoot through ice-packed trails to Communist camps. Those who couldn't keep up were shot.

These are the atrocities of one side.

They are the only atrocities my father allows.

But if we start the story sooner – in the 1930s rather than December 1944 – we see a different progression. In the 1930s, Greece was ruled by a dictator who suspended Parliament, outlawed the Communist Party, censored the press, and sponsored the torture of Communist citizens.

This could be the beginning.

Or, alternatively, the beginning could be found in the 1920s, when Greece underwent thirteen changes of government – coups, countercoups, elections nullified – in fifteen years. Stuck inside this stuttering backwardness, Greece needed a strong leader to unite the country as the worldwide war approached.

He was an officer in the dictator's army.

He, Agamemnon Apostolides, my grandfather: he was a high-ranking officer in the Cavalry Division, an army veterinarian who coordinated the deployment of 40,000 pack animals – animals that were vital to the army's transportation system. Greece had no airplanes, and very few tanks and trucks. It had, instead, horses and mules. If the army wanted to transport food to the soldiers; if it needed to get bandages, scalpels, antiseptics to doctors at the front; if the government decided to remove the injured from the battlefield, or the dead: all this was done by pack animal. Horses, mules, donkeys and, on occasion, village women.

A veterinarian was essential.

Agamemnon.

Agamemnon was loyal to the dictator; he believed in the

rule of law.

Agamemnon did not believe in torture, nor did he seek its evidence.

Agamemnon rose through the ranks. He was hanged in a barn.

This was Round One (1942–1944), when Communist guerrillas attacked the Axis occupiers. The Communists wanted to free Greece from Nazi rule; they wanted to rule Greece once it was free. With these goals in mind, the Communists attacked the Axis indiscriminately; their Conservative countrymen, they targeted.

Tap-tap.

The Conservatives beheaded Communist leaders and stuck their heads on wooden poles. They danced through the streets, jubilating around the freshly impaled head. This was Round Three of the Greek Civil War (1945–1949).

Round Two (December 1944) was the fighting in Athens, when government forces secured themselves atop the Acropolis, hiding behind the ancient stones, training their rifles on the Communists below.

One, two, three: Where do we begin.

Where do I begin with this story?

"So what do you do when this man shouts Communist slogans?"

"You blended. You blended in the background: you learned how to do that. The less you were noticed, the better it was."

"So you –"

"So you were a non entity."

Tap the ring.

Now round the obstacle, avoiding contact. Sense it beside

you and skim around, but do not touch or you will lose. Now move, fast.

Now tell me a story.

&

"We were going to the village. Laspiti was driving the cart and I was in the middle. It was a pleasant drive – a couple of hours on dirt roads and what have you. And we were passing a meadow. At the end of the meadow was a hedge that separated one farm from the other. And against that hedge was a lady with a red dress. She was sitting down, wearing a broad-rimmed hat with a flower. She was an older woman. She was sitting on the ground, feet out, wearing short black heels. And Laspiti said, 'Well, she's gone. I wonder when anybody will pick her up.'"

She wore a flower in her hat.

She was older, wearing black shoes and a red dress.

"It was like, 'Oh my God, is she dead?' Because I was kind of hoping she wouldn't be dead. I thought, you know, that maybe she just sat down to take a rest."

They were heading toward the village where Agamemnon would treat the farmers' animals: horses and cows, mules and goats. These animals were vital to the community's survival. Without healthy animals, the village couldn't feed itself; without my grandfather, the animals wouldn't be healthy. Everyone knew the power Agamemnon possessed.

"People came running over, calling to dad: 'My cow's having problems – can you have a look after you finish with this horse?' 'And my horse has an abscess! Can you treat the abscess?' And then it became an event; people would come just to say hello and talk politics. He'd be treating one animal, and suddenly there'd be forty people watching."

The communists were watching, too.

"It's frightening, if you're a little kid."

"What's frightening? Being in the villages? Because of the Communists?"

"No, no: they didn't bother us – not usually."

"What's frightening then?"

I'm confused: I haven't followed the movement of his thoughts; I haven't connected these parts of the story.

They are not a story.

"The woman," he says.

"Which woman?"

The woman with the red dress, sitting by the side of the road.

"Because you hear, 'She's gone,' but you don't believe it. On the way back from the village – seven or eight hours later – you're in the cart, heading home on the same dirt road."

This is twenty minutes later on the interview tape.

"And you keep looking," he says. "You're looking and looking and waiting to get to that spot, to *get* to that spot…. And then you think: Maybe she was sleeping, because she's not there – she's not against that hedge…. She's not there, she's not there…. And then you think: Maybe she got up and went home! But then you look, and there she is – and it's exactly the same, and it hasn't changed – so you know that she's dead….

"And these are the scenes that changed your attitude," he says. "These are the things you saw that made you turn inward, not express yourself, become more afraid. 'Can this happen to me? Can I walk down the street and drop dead and be there for days in a row? And nobody would care?'"

These are the scenes in his life.

This is not a 'scene' in literature.

There are no scenes; there is no narrative – beginning and end, cause-and-effect, climax and denouement. There are, instead, details.

An Adam's apple. A broad-rimmed hat. A metal ring.

There are objects, excised from any progression.

A boy in rags; forty people in a circle.

These are memories.

And this is how we play the game. He gives me memories – an image or sensation, a physical moment – and I construct a scene. I make, of him, a work of literature.

༄

"Have you heard about the Americans? Are they going to win the war for us?"

The farmers stood in a circle around Agamemnon and the horse. Their drawstring pants and buttoned shirts stank from their days in the fields; their sweat had soaked the fabric and then evaporated, leaving only an odour that became sharper as the days passed. The villagers had gathered on a patch of grass outside the house. The manure pile was alive with flies.

"I don't think it will be that simple," Agamemnon said. He bent to examine the horse's injury. His fingers probed the swollen leg. When he reached one particular spot, the animal swung its neck and bellowed. "It's okay," Agamemnon commanded. He eased a finger back and forth above the ankle joint, feeling the fluid that pooled inside the tissue.

"How long has the animal been limping?" he asked the farmer.

"Two days, doctor. Two or three."

"And was there a specific injury – a blow or a twist?"

"Not that I know of. There might have been, of course."

"Of course."

Taki stood beside his father, unseen in the centre of everything.

"Taki," Agamemnon said. "I need you to build a fire. Get the matches from my bag. The rod, too."

Agamemnon had explained this procedure to Taki once before: the rod would be held over a fire until it became sufficiently hot, at which point it would be placed directly on the horse's injured limb. The rod would bring heat, which would bring blood, which would remove the toxins that caused the limp: this was the theory.

"It'll take a moment before we begin," Agamemnon told the farmer.

Taki searched the ground for dry sticks.

"What do you think of this EAM/ELAS, doctor?" one farmer asked. "I hear they want to attack the Nazis. They say we can be proud again."

"I don't think it's a question of 'pride' when it comes to the Nazis."

"But they blew up a bridge, not far from here. And the Nazis, they couldn't move their trucks for hours. The trucks just sat there – these huge machines stopped by one little bomb! Just one little thing! That's all we have – one little thing. But we're *smart*," the farmer said, tapping his temple. "The Greeks are *smart*. We stopped them with *nothing*. That takes guts –

real manliness."

Agamemnon shrugged. "I don't know. It was certainly very showy." He was scrubbing his hands in the stone fountain.

"I guess it's showy," the farmer said. "But what a show!" He looked around for confirmation, nodding to his fellow villagers. "A good show, wasn't it?"

Agamemnon coughed two times, precisely.

Taki had been taught how to build a fire in the Boy Scouts. He arranged the sticks in a pyramid, leaving a hatching of holes. A fire needs air – it breathes air like a person, the Boy Scouts' leader had said. He'd been killed at Koritsa; the Boy Scout troop hadn't reassembled. Taki lit the fire.

"The trucks were there for *hours*."

"Hours. Interesting. Tell me, did you have a plan for responding to the attack, assuming the Nazis had come to the village? Assuming they'd asked for the names of the men who'd set the bomb?"

"No, but…" The man puffed up his cheeks, then popped out the air audibly. "I mean, the men weren't *from* this village."

"Do you think the Nazis care?"

"I guess not, but –"

"So what was the plan?"

A woman waved her arm now, the muscle stringy on the bone. "I heard the Nazis shot eight men in Klissoura," she said. "Innocent men, with children! Shot them in the *platia* – boom!" She clapped her hands together – *boom* – a brisk slap, quick and done.

Agamemnon began to cleanse the horse's leg with alcohol. He glanced at the villagers as they argued. Some said the Greeks would betray their heritage if they did nothing against the Axis. "And not just the ancients! But the fallen heroes of Epirus, too!" one said. "May they rest in peace," he added. Several people made the sign of the cross.

"There won't be any peace if we kill a Nazi soldier!" a woman responded, her voice nasal and piercing.

"She's right. Did you hear about the new law? The Nazis said they'll –"

The villagers shouted across the circle at each other, their voices intersecting. Agamemnon let them yell. He was the only one who was truly listening, hearing the themes of various arguments, the perspectives that got tangled in this war.

"Doctor," one man called. "Doctor, what do *you* think we should do?"

"What should we do?" Agamemnon said. He'd finished arranging his tools on a tray, placing scalpels and razors in two straight rows. "We should strengthen our communities – take care of our own. Keep ourselves fed, educated. And we should leave the Germans alone – they won't be here forever. And *we* can't defeat them by ourselves. This war is happening all over the world. A few of us here – we can't defeat them."

A young man sniggered. He wore his beard long, his hair curly on his forehead. Agamemnon didn't recognize him. He paused, assessing. He then chose a razor and shaved the hair off the horse's ankle; he ran the blade upward, revealing the animal's stark-white skin. "Tell me," he said, glancing back at the man. "Tell me: What do *you* think we should do?"

"We should attack them," the man said, without hesitation. "We can't defeat the Germans – you're right about that. But we *can* slow them down. We can cost them money." He brushed the hair off his face. "We can kill some." Along his forehead was a white scar, the dead skin knitted together in an uneven seam. The wound had not been clean; it had been caused by a sudden accident, Agamemnon thought, or a careful calculation.

"We can kill some Germans, true," Agamemnon responded. "And then they'll kill some of us."

"It's a war. People die in wars."

Agamemnon wiped the blade on his thigh, removing the horse's hairs. "What's your name?" he asked.

"Aleko Alexiou."

Agamemnon nodded. This was the son of a local farmer, the boy who'd been imprisoned for his Communist activities.

"And what's yours?" Aleko asked.

Agamemnon laid the razor on the tray. "I'm Dr. Agamemnon Apostolides."

"Yes," Aleko said. "I've heard of you."

By now, the rod had absorbed the flame into itself, assuming its colour and lustre. Taki watched the red glow seep up the rod.

"I've treated your father's animals," Agamemnon replied.

Aleko shook his head, not breaking his gaze. "No. That's not how I know your name."

༒

He remembers details. Their progression holds inside his body; their sinew is his form. From these memories – these sensations with their correspondence and relation – my father's body moves.

There is no distinction: his history, his body, the words that he tells me.

I shape a story.

My father is seventy-two but trim and fit, agile in his movements. He swims in a pool, dozens of laps each day. I watch him now emerge from the water. The hair is silver around his nipples; his belly is striated with muscle. This is the body that holds his story.

He gives me details and I construct a scene.

I construct a scene that fails.

"Tell me," Agamemnon said, *"did you have a plan for responding…"*

It's *fake!* These words are *false!* I am *frustrated* by this page – my words, this scene – this is an evisceration! I sever his story from physical truth; I kill what was once alive.

This is fiction: organize the scene, make the characters clear; help the reader to move from one moment to the next.

But the moments do not come like that! The moments come like blood from a wound, too fast for me to capture.

How do you capture the blood that pulses in your father?

How do I contain this story?

"Should we continue?" I ask.

His biceps are beautifully defined.

∽

November 15, 1940

My Dearest Mary,

I just received your letter from the 4th. I was so happy with your good news. I hope it will be followed by a calm life, and that all these small adventures, and the continuous fear in our hearts, will be only memories.

Today is sunny and beautiful. The lake is shining, totally clear. There are very few civilians walking about. Although this is a big, beautiful city, it has the appearance of a cemetery. All the residents are hiding deep in caves. All you can see are army personnel walking toward the front lines. With God's help, the murderous Italians will learn what it means to confront the Greeks.

To Loukaki: I thank her a lot because she wrote me a beautiful letter. Why didn't Taki do the same? It seems that he's not reading as much as he should, and he doesn't write. Although one little birdie *did* tell me that he was behaving right, and I love him and kiss him on both cheeks. I want him and Loukia to kiss Yiayia and Papou on my behalf. And in the next letter, I want Taki to write me a note – how he is, and whether he is studying.

Here the weather is very cold, especially at night, and I must cover my head with blankets. Mary, there's such a variety of climate here, you can't imagine. It would be wonderful for us to make changes in our lives – to see different kinds of life and different people. You totally change your outlook when you are here.

Now, because I am tired, I am ending this letter. I kiss you all – you, Taki and Loukia.

Love,
Memnon

This letter has been translated by my aunt, Loukia, because my father is unable to decipher his father's handwriting. He holds a stack of letters, which he hasn't seen since they arrived, one at a time, in November 1940 through April 1941, when Greece was fighting the Italians.

My grandmother brought these letters across the Atlantic, tucked inside the single trunk that she carried from Greece. For sixty years, she kept them always underneath her bed, tied with twine.

"It's very frustrating to be looking at these letters without being able to understand them," he says. His voice is devoid of frustration; it's devoid of any emotion at all. "It's like they're written in code."

"Do you remember receiving the letters?"

"No."

"Do you remember saying goodbye when your father went to the front?"

"No."

"Do you –"

"I don't remember any of that. I can see my father, but I don't remember him. He's kind of there, but he's kind of in a fog. He doesn't come into focus as a sharp personality."

"As a person."

"As a man."

☙

He speaks in themes. If I listen, I hear them.

From these, I must shape a story – a vessel that holds the absolute truth – a truth which is conveyed without ever being said.

He remembers moments; he tells me details; he speaks in themes.

I must listen; I must hear what he does not say.

He taps the ring. I state the theme. We play the game.

ɕʓ

"Good day, Mrs. Apostolides," says the man outside the window. It is a different man, but the message will be the same. "Your husband sends his love."

Taki's knees are tucked up, his arms encircling his legs. His chin is sliding on the kneecap, bone-on-bone separated by the thinnest layers of skin. A black band is sewn on his shirt sleeve. It had been removed and re-sewn three times in the past two months, changing with each visit: *he's alive, he's dead; he's alive, he's dead; he's alive.*

He's dead.

The last visit was ten days earlier, when Laspiti came to the door. He was holding a watermelon, as if the family could eat after hearing his news. "Is your mother home?" he asked Taki, ruffling the boy's curly hair – black like his father's had been.

"I don't –"

"Send him away!" his mother screamed, running forward. "He's like the ravens, feasting on us!" She grappled with Laspiti, who offered no resistance. She hurled the watermelon onto the front steps. "Tell him to bring me a *body* to mourn! Don't bring me *rumours*, bring me a *body!* Tell him, Taki!"

Taki looked at Laspiti.

"She says –"

"I heard, Taki…. You don't need to say it."

Although Taki had been hungry that day, he didn't attempt to retrieve the chunks of watermelon. He sat in the window instead, listening to his mother wail; he watched as the birds ate the pink fruit.

Taki is hungry now, too, but this man doesn't bring watermelon. This man, like the other Communist rebels, asks for things: boots or scalpels or syringes. These objects will assist Agamemnon, they say. Agamemnon is, they emphasize, a hostage – a *vital* hostage, a *valued* hostage – a man captured because of his unparalleled veterinary skills. Agamemnon will remain in their camps, treating their animals, until the enemy – the Nazi invaders – have been defeated. At that time, the Communists say, Agamemnon will be returned home.

"He requests his stethoscope," this man adds. He maintains a respectful distance from Taki's mother. "He says you'll know where to find it."

"Yes!"

Taki sits beside the window, hidden by the sun's glare off the clear glass. He stares at the man, the Communist who stands at the threshold of their house. His hair is stiff, unwashed and coarsened by life in the guerrilla camp. He scratches at it, glimpsing the medical plaque beside the door: the serpents intertwined around a staff. He smiles. An eye tooth is missing but otherwise his smile is bone-white against the dirt of his face. Taki stares. This is a member of ELAS. This is a Communist. This, stiff and hard, with a gun handle hooked in his waistband: this abducted his father.

His mother returns with a bag. "Please give him my note, too," she begs. "You will, won't you?"

"Of course, Mrs. Apostolides. We always do." He takes her hand and kisses her fingers, his lips on the gold wedding band. He turns from the house, tossing back his hair. Before descending, he winks, quick, directly at Taki.

One drop of urine blots Taki's pants.

જી

"You really believed he was alive? Even though Laspiti told you he was dead?"

"Of course! Laspiti *told* us he was dead, but so what! What does that mean! We had no body, Marianne. We had no physical evidence. Of *course* we believed he was alive!"

"For over a year? For all that time, you thought –"

"Did it make *sense* that they used him as a veterinarian? Yes, it made sense. Did you *want* to believe he was alive? Yes, you wanted to believe. Of course."

Of course they believed: the story was plausible, logical. Agamemnon possessed rare and precious knowledge; the Communists needed this knowledge; therefore, they kept him alive. This story makes sense.

"And I think a lot of my resentment comes from that continuous emotional rollercoaster. You know: up and down – he's alive, he's dead; he's alive, he's dead. You know, it left me…" His voice quavers. "It's kind of interesting," he says, regaining control.

"It left you…?"

"My feelings were kind of dead for a long time."

જી

The ring came from a wooden barrel that carried wine; the barrel's slats were permeated by a purplish odour. But the ring itself – a metal strip encircling the outside, holding the barrel into shape – that was impervious.

Tap the ring.

They had no wine in the 1940s: no wine, no meat and very little bread. But in the 1930s, Agamemnon and Mary drank fine Cabernet and waltzed with their friends from the army. The room where they danced had a frescoed ceiling: sky blue with puffed white clouds, fresh-faced cherubs clustered together, aiming their arrows down. Agamemnon's favorite composer was Strauss.

"Do you remember any happy moments from those years? Anything wonderful that happened?"

"You know, that sense of doing what you *have* to do – doing only what you *have* to do and staying out of trouble: it's still there today!"

This awareness seems to startle him. He rises to it, suddenly angered. "It shapes your life, and your character. That was the overwhelming sense and emotion for me: you must do what you have to do…. I *had* to do this and I *had* to do that and I *had* to do this and I *had* to do that; I went from one thing to the other to the other to the next and I never stopped to develop a…"

"A what?"

"Happy moments?" he replies, reverting to the original question. "No, there weren't any happy, carefree moments, where *you* did what you wanted to do. Where you did something that wasn't rehearsed."

He's forgotten an entire way he was. Not just moments – scenes – but sensations, engagements: him in the world, in his body, with others. He dismisses my question as if it were irrelevant to his story.

"No, Marianne: I don't remember a spontaneous moment of any type."

I want to change what is relevant.

I will choose what pertains.

He got caught in a tide.

"I remember!"

He'd been swimming off the pier with his best friend, Nikos Hadzis. They were fifteen years old, exploring a Nazi warship that was half-sunken, left behind when the Germans made their hasty retreat from Greece. But while the boys explored this man-made island, the tide was turning; as they attempted to swim ashore, they were carried north. "So we had to crawl out in somebody's backyard!"

His laughter is an overflow, a shiver through his body. "*Thimame!*" he repeats as Nikos laughs.

"*Thimame* – I remember!"

Nikos and my father had walked back home, sopping wet in their black bathing suits and bare chests. They strolled through the centre of town – the fancy part, with expensive shops frequented by well-dressed ladies who wore jewels and summer hats.

He laughs.

He must've felt it then: his youth. A young man with broadening shoulders, slender hips like his father. Ideal. An ideal Greek man, trim but muscular – agile, able to respond. He walked, watched by the ladies in their summer dresses; he and Nikos goaded each other, transgressing the rules, striding down the fancy street.

He giggles, overflowing.

He hasn't spoken with Nikos in 53 years.

"I remember his walk," he says that night when Nikos goes home. "I mean, he's still the same guy. Oh, he's changed – he's fifty years older! His face has changed, but not that much! If I saw him – if I saw him on the street – I would say, 'I *know* that man. But from *where?*'"

We arrived in Greece three hours earlier. My father has not been here since he emigrated in 1949. He finds Nikos' name in Thessaloniki's phone book. "Don't go anywhere," Nikos commanded. "I'm coming over, right now. Don't go anywhere, okay Taki?"

They talked for hours; they promised to keep in touch.

That was ten years ago.

Now: now we tap the ring and circle back. We come to the end and change direction, turning in a tight reverse. If we stand on the inside, the ring will arc around, drawing a boundary. This will keep us contained.

Stand contained. This allows more control.

I don't want control.

"*Thimame!*" he said.

I've never heard that sound from him. His laughter has never possessed that tone – that gorgeous, voluptuous overflow.

I remember: I will choose.

℘

They stripped the body. They hanged him in a barn then stripped the clothes from the corpse.

They wore my dead grandfather's clothing.

This detail he did not know.

He knew the shrapnel, the watermelon, the metal ring.

This, though: this he didn't know to remember.

"You never *told* us," he says. He is seventy years old; we are sipping wine in the village where his father was killed. He is here because I've asked him for his story. "You should've told us about the clothes."

Constantia Laspiti sits on her veranda, gazing toward the foothills. Her hair is greasy; her eyes are opaque with cataracts.

"You never told us," he repeats, though Laspiti's wife speaks no English. She rocks in her chair, hugging her fleshy arms.

The killer, he learns, rode his horse into the village just after the murder. He headed to Laspiti's house, where Agamemnon's clothing would be recognized. Constantia was there, working in her garden; she was six months' pregnant.

'Who will baptize your baby now?' the man asked.

'Agamemnon Apostolides!'

The man adjusted the collar on Agamemnon's shirt.

'Agamemnon Apostolides!' Constantia insisted, panicked.

The man made his horse rear up, near Constantia's pregnant belly.

'Agamemnon Apostolides,' he said, 'is dead.'

"If we had known…"

Constantia can't comprehend my father's words.

He speaks, nonetheless, aloud.

I listen.

The killer stripped the body. In order to do so, his fingers must've executed delicate movements, an intimate contact: a button through the slit in the fabric, the body still supple. The killer must've stripped his own body, too, taking off his pants and shirt, tossing them onto the hay. They were naked, both men – chest, nipples, bruises, scars – naked in the barn, the noose cut down, the truncated rope swaying.

Tap the ring; complete the circle.

"You never told us…. I wish you'd told us…."

She looks toward the foothills. She will be dead in two months.

∽

He cried only once. In seven years of interviews – seventy-three hours of interview tape, one trip to Greece, thirty-four discrete interview sessions – my father cried only once.

"They were the saddest-looking group," he says, describing the last German phalanx that marched through the city as the Nazis fled the Allied advance. "But they were still the stiff upper lip, marching to the drum."

As the Germans retreated, the Communists gathered on the outskirts of Thessaloniki, preparing to claim their victory. This was the day – the moment – they'd see their father again.

"There must've been a phalanx of six or eight deep and they were walking down the centre of the city. They had a drummer and he was beating a march, and they were marching down the block."

They believed they'd see him. They anticipated his arrival. Waiting indoors, they watched the Germans marching.

"And the city was absolutely empty. Absolutely empty. Not a soul, you couldn't hear anything. You just heard the drum."

"What are you feeling when you're watching the Germans?"

"Well, because of our experiences, we had no idea what

was going to happen. I mean, everybody was very happy to see them leave. But, with me, it was like: 'Now the Communists are coming out of hiding with their hostages. So now we'll know.'"

He was alone. His sister was with their mother, asking her to braid her hair. She wanted to look beautiful for her father, she said.

"So after the Germans were gone, a kid rode a bicycle up and down the street shouting, 'The last German has left! Now you can come out!' And the whole city was instantly in the streets, screaming and yelling and welcoming the Communists as liberators. And down they came from the mountains in a huge parade."

The Freedom Day Parade.

"What did you do? When everybody's cheering?"

"I avoided the celebrations, because I was very apprehensive. But excited, too."

"Because you believed he was alive."

"Because I believed, right. So I climbed the gate in front of our house. From there, I could see all the heads of everyone who passed."

"And you waited there?"

"I waited all day."

For seven hours, he sat on that gate. He watched as hordes of men paraded, greeted by cheers and admiration. He sat. He waited. For hours, he searched, seeking the face of his father; searching, looking at thousands of men – thousands of faces – beseeching, asking one of them to look back. To see him there, waiting.

Tap the ring.

"You know, Marianne," he said, "they were all killed."

"Who?"

"That last German contingent. They got out of town and marched right into an ambush. The Communists killed them. Every one of them. All those young boys going home."

And this is when he cries.

 ❧

When he came to America in August 1949, my father didn't have a name.

His teachers at Far Rockaway High School on Long Island, New York didn't know what to label this boy. This 'Efstratios' Apostolides, nicknamed 'Taki.'

"Stanley," one teacher said. "Your name will be Stanley."

"Yes," he said, comprehending nothing except the laughter. "Yes."

'Stanley' didn't stick. In the winter, another teacher suggested 'Strait' since 'Strat' for Ef-*strat*-ios didn't sound good to her. "Strait is better than Strat, don't you think? Don't you think... hello? Hello... Stanley?"

"Yes."

They laughed and laughed, and he laughed too: it was all so funny here, in North America.

He laughed and the heater clunked on, warming the insides of his thighs.

'Strait' became Steve except Steve stood for 'Stavros' and Taki was Efstratios, so 'Steve' didn't last.

'Dimitri' was offered since Dimitri was Greek.

But Taki wasn't merely Greek, he was 'Taki,' Efstrataki, Efstratios, son of Agamemnon and Mary, grandson of Efstratios and Loukia, of Yiorgos and Evantheia, born in Thessaloniki, Greece in 1933, before the war, when he was among the elite.

"Hey Dimitri, have you ever seen a car before? *Vroom vroom!* A car? Ever see one?"

"Yes."

He didn't tell them about the tanks or airplanes, the Nazi Jeeps, the men with waistbands bulging with guns barely hidden.

Vroom, vroom.

'James' was suggested by his boss at the Esso station, where he pumped gas.

"James?"

"Yes."

'James' can't be pronounced in Greek.

In the fall of 1950, James made the Dean's List at high school. One year later, he attended a local college, then applied to Cornell University Veterinary School. In the subsequent decades, Dr. James Apostolides, DVM, married a first-generation Greek-American, established a veterinary hospital on Long Island, fathered a boy (who became a lawyer) and a girl (who became a writer). In all those years, James never told anyone about his childhood. Then, in December 1998, his daughter invited him to Toronto. She wanted to write a book about his childhood, she explained; she thought this process – the construction of scenes, a narrative, a single cohesive story – could 'release him' from the trauma of his past. She couldn't admit to her deeper desire: that his release would be her own.

She held the pen; he tapped the ring.

And in this time – in the decade in which she grappled with her father's past – she learned that his story could never release her: a story will always fail to cohere.

The insistent freedom produced by this realization surprises her.

∾

"And there was one incident I remember with Laspiti," he tells me. "There was a cart, and he brought the horse to the cart – it was a beautiful horse, he was very proud of that horse. Anyway, he wanted to back the horse into the cart, and it wouldn't go." My father wipes his lips. "You know, it was always awkward for a horse to back up. They would twitch their tails and raise their hooves. But usually they'd go – they'd back up into the cart – but this one wouldn't. And Laspiti got so upset. He had a crop and he started to hit him on the belly. *'You do as I tell you!'* BAM! *'Do as I say!'* And then he said, 'Now you back up.'

"And the horse did. He backed up. I was so impressed by that."

"Why were you impressed?"

"The way he interacted with his horse. Here he was: a loving man, a smart man, getting very upset. And he was proud of that animal – it was a beautiful horse, a muscular horse. And he asserted himself. And when he did, the animal responded." My father pauses, smiles, as if bemused. "Now why do you remember something like that?" he asks.

"There must be a reason."

Tap the ring. Take it home, as best you can.

What We Do for Money

George bought me a drink that afternoon. He jerked himself onto a stool, wiped the sweat from his forehead and jowls. "This is Tammy," he said, introducing me to the bartender.

"Pleasure," Tammy offered, extending her hand.

Tammy had worked as a prostitute for three years, George explained; she'd switched jobs the previous month, when she was fitted with a mouthful of braces.

Tammy smiled silver and poured two shots – sweet brown liquid that cracked the cubes of ice. "It'll take me years to pay the orthodontist bills," she said, "considering the tips I get here."

George flung her a twenty.

"Thanks, Georgie." She winked and smiled, slipping the bill in the back pocket of her jeans. The fabric parted for her fingers.

George turned toward me, proposing a toast to college girls. I clinked his glass and pretended to drink, letting the liquid flow close to my lips. I didn't really consume alcohol at that point in my life. I didn't consume food, either – not in public, anyway. "Lord love college girls," George said, exhaling the fumes of Scotch. "Amen!"

I wore stretch pants that day and a boxy-cut blazer, a fashion choice based solely on the fact that those particular garments fit me on that particular day. I was a virgin: a bulimic, virgin, Princeton undergraduate writing about commercial sex from a purely legal perspective.

Purely.

"College girls and Scotch: oh Lord, oh yes! A beautiful combination, don't you think? What do you think, Tammy?"

"I think all girls are beautiful, George."

"Amen!"

Beyond the bar was a vast lobby ringed with couches on which various women lounged about. Some wore lingerie; others sat in jeans and button-down blouses. Many knitted or busied themselves with nail files and polish. She was reading trash – romantic, tragic, a story swollen with bad writing – but I imagined it to be otherwise.

She was beautiful.

The lobby of the Mustang Ranch, this most illustrious brothel in the illustrious state of Nevada, was fed by a single narrow hallway. This was where the men entered from the dusty parking lot, as one was entering now. A buzzer blared to announce his arrival. The women rose from the couches and formed a line across the carpet. From my spot at the bar, I could see only their backs.

Hers was strong – two columns of muscle rounding toward her spine. She leaned her weight on one leg, thumbs hooked into the waistband of her pants. They were blue pants, Capri-style. Her tank top was tight, striped in red and cream, cropped at the last rib. While she awaited the man's decision, she shook her hair out of its twist. The tips brushed against her skin, low down, where the back arches all of its own.

The man took in the abundance of women aligned before him – all those limbs and torsos and breasts and lips. The Mustang's Madame, older and elegant, spoke to the man with comforting guidance. He nodded, looked to her face, then back to the line up, his left knee bobbing. The Madame laid one hand on his shoulder and swept the other through the air, displaying the options. The women didn't twitter or vamp. They stood. She stood. She gathered her hair – straight and long and chestnut brown – over one shoulder. She waited.

"I bet he comes to the bar first," George said. "Lots of times they come to the bar first. They have a drink, relax, get to talking with a lady."

"They leave shitty tips," Tammy said.

George retrieved his billfold. He dangled a twenty between two fingers, making Tammy come and get it, which she did.

The man at the door pointed to a woman in a pink teddy covered by a faux-silk robe, the belt undone.

"I was wrong," George said, observing.

"You don't know how to read 'em."

"That's not my job."

The other girls resumed their positions on the couches. The woman with the tank top touched her forefinger to her tongue and turned the page of her book. I thought she might have looked briefly toward the bar, toward me, but I'm not sure: I didn't look back.

The ice was melting in my drink.

George squeezed my hand, his fingers fleshy, and told me to wait right there. He huffed off the stool, pumping his arms to get himself moving. George was a gargantuan man. He drove a wide white Cadillac and wore well-tailored white suits – luxuries afforded by the proceeds of his White Bell Chapel, which offered drive-thru weddings seven days a week. Yes, George was my ticket in. He was the spokesman for the Nevada Brothels' Association, a beloved figure in the state's thirty-three legal cathouses. I'd contacted him from Princeton, hoping he could clarify his stance regarding the benefits and shortfalls of the legalized brothel system. George had responded by inviting me out west. He could show me around, he'd said; he could show me a good time.

"Wait right there, baby." I didn't expect to feel so nervous without the bulk of him beside me.

I stirred my drink, thankful for the activity. The buzzer blared. The women lined up. I tapped the plastic stir-stick against the rim of the glass – *tap-tap* – and there was nothing more to do. I straightened my spine. The buzzer blared. The women lined up: she was gone. No sheet of chestnut hair, no bare back low down. I gripped my glass. I was at a bar in a brothel, by myself, with no one to talk to, a drink sweating in my hand. I gulped the Scotch. The buzzer blared.

Across from me, at the other end of the bar, a prostitute chatted with a youngish man, beefy-large, his linebacker muscles turning to fat. The prostitute was Raedene – Raedene from rural Oregon – somebody's version of pretty. George had introduced us earlier in the afternoon. Raedene had told me the same story I'd heard all week, from dozens of prostitutes in cathouses across the state: prostitution was a good job, she'd said. She made good money, met interesting men, controlled her own working life. And sex, she'd added, had very little to do with it. "I'm an actress and a therapist," she'd said as I scribbled some notes, "and a mind-reader and an independent contractor." She'd blinked then, smiling with relief that she'd remembered the whole list. "Besides," she'd giggled, "it sure beats cleaning toilets in some casino downtown!"

Raedene's breath had smelled heavily of peppermint mouthwash.

Raedene and the man weren't at the bar anymore. She must be acting on her bed, I thought. Or independently negotiating a new contract, or administering therapy without a license. Or... what was the fourth? I couldn't remember the fourth.... Actress ... therapist ... I licked my lips which tingled with an unfamiliar wide-alive numbness. The feeling didn't get washed away by my tongue. I wasn't sure whether I liked it there.

"She's waiting for you, honey."

George's hand was on my back. He leaned in close, his mouth on my ear. "Room 14, baby. She's waiting for you."

"Room –"

"Go on. She's waiting."

I walked down the motel-like hallway, uncertain where I was headed. Room 14. Raedene fluttered out of Room 8, cash in hand. She winked at me, her sky-blue eyeshadow expertly applied, her lipstick now faded. Room 8, 10, 12....

The door was open just slightly – just enough – and her bed was empty.

"Hello?" I ventured.

"Sit down." She was curled on the room's only chair. I shuffled, awkward, looking for someplace to sit. "There," she said. She pointed at the bed.

"Of course!" I said. I was sweating through my blazer. "Sorry, I –"

"Don't apologize," she replied; it was a command, not a kindness. "George said you've got questions."

"Yes, I –"

"You've got half-an-hour. Paid for." She glanced at one of four clocks that hung on the wall.

"Paid?"

"George."

"Oh, but I…!"

George often bought time with the girls – not for talking, of course. "I didn't ask him to buy me –"

"He didn't buy *you* anything," she said.

"He bought –"

"Do you have questions for me? Or not."

"I do," I answered. "I do…." I sat on the bed, as told. I retrieved my Princeton folder which contained a list of fourteen questions, all vetted by my thesis advisor weeks in advance. "I'd like to begin with the basics," I said, reading primly off the page. "What brought you here?"

"What brought *you* here?"

"Um… I'm writing my thesis on the legalization of prostitution."

"And I'm getting out of debt. Next question."

"Next question…" I fumbled with my papers, dense with all those bullet-pointed, pre-approved words:

- *Start with the basics: What brought you to the brothels? Do you have any complaints about working here? Describe a typical day.*
- *Why, specifically, did you 'choose' to become a prostitute? What other 'choices' did you have?*

- *What is/are the fundamental difference(s) between legal brothel prostitution and street-walking?*
- *What (really) are you selling? Sexual services? Body? Self? Can there (really) be boundaries between them?*

"You're wasting time," she eventually said.

"I know, I…" I set the papers on the mattress. "I've interviewed a lot of women who say it's not about sex," I said. I flushed at speaking the word, to her, on her bed.

"Really," she responded. "That's what they say?"

"They tell me –"

But she didn't let me finish. She thrust her feet on the floor and slid to the edge of her chair. She leaned toward me, pelvis pressed down. "This…" she said, then paused.

"Yes?" I stared at her eyes – only her eyes as she swiveled her shoulders.

"This… " she repeated, "is most definitely about sex."

My breath released – a small moan – and her contempt spread over me, thick.

"Yeah, it's about sex. But anyway," she sighed, "I touch them as little as possible."

She sat back, relaxed again, legs curled up. She'd gotten good at her job, she said as she toyed with the hem of her blue Capri pants. She could read the signals: a certain scent in the sweat or dryness to the mouth; a certain rhythm to their breathing. She watched me and smiled. She paused just long enough for fresh sweat to spurt from my pores. She could get the Johns primed, she concluded, simply by talking – by taking them right to the edge so she barely had to touch them at all.

"But then you have to touch them," I said, my forehead now pulsing from the Scotch.

She guffawed. "Yeah. Then I have to touch them." She shook out her hair. She stretched her shoulders back, one hand on the roped muscle of her neck, rubbing. "Do you have any other questions?" She looked at me now. Her body became still – eyes, mouth, gaze – tautly still except her fingers, which circled. "Is there anything else you want to know."

"I want to know," I said. I swallowed viscous saliva; my breath was uneven. "I want to know what happens after... if... when you touch them."

She cackled, hard.

"I mean...!"

And what else could she do, really? What was the appropriate response to such an asinine question from a twenty-one-year-old bulimic virgin co-ed from an East Coast Ivy League school whose best strategy for learning about sex was to write her thesis about prostitution?

"What happens to you," I whispered. "What happens to *you* when you touch them."

At that, the woman (so beautiful), she laughed again. But the sound was different now. This was the laughter of surprise – genuine, lovely, unscripted surprise. "To me?"

"To you."

"Me?" She closed her mouth, jaw tensed, her gentleness fleeing. "To *me*?" She purred, she growled. "Me... I lose a little of myself. Every time."

I looked at her – her tank top and skin, her fingers that circled. I looked and removed my jacket.

One revelation demanded another.

48

My shoulders were contoured, lush but muscular. I was strong. With my body as the place of embattlement, I needed to be strong: this was where my power lay, inside its desire; this was where I needed to give my brutality.

"What do you mean?" I asked. "Explain it to me. I'd like to listen."

"You'd like to listen to *me*?"

"I'd like to hear your thoughts."

"You'd like to hear *my* thoughts?"

"Please," I said, a directive not a plea – not completely.

"You've got eighteen minutes left," she asserted.

"Then give me eighteen minutes."

"Fuck," she breathed, looking at a clock.

"It's paid for," I added.

"It always is."

For the next eighteen minutes, she wrestled with her thoughts as we wrestled with each other. I pushed and she engaged but then withdrew, and I pursued. And then she engaged again. She wanted to explain, I think. She wanted to understand her own metaphor, her story; I definitely wanted to elicit it.

"I still don't understand how you 'lose yourself.' You say you 'lose yourself,' but you haven't told me how."

"I feel like... after two years of working here, it's like..." She made a fist and held it up; it shook from the force of her clenching. "It's like I get so small every time I do a job. It's like I go into this little room right here." She put her fist to her belly, beneath her sternum, pushing in. "And I can't come back out anymore. I'm getting stuck in there. I feel..."

She stopped.

"Tell me what you feel," I said. "What do you feel, trapped in that space. Can you tell me?"

"Every time a man comes in my mouth or my cunt, it's like…"

"Keep going: please. Tell me what it's like."

And she struck her fist into the air, springing toward me. *"Tell me,"* she mimicked, her voice mincing. *"Tell me! Tell me!"* I leaned back, my body on the bed. *"Tell me what's it's like to be a whore: I really want to know."*

"I –"

She was bent over me now, pinning me down without contact. "I'll tell you something, little girl…"

I felt us breathing, her chest close to mine. Her hair was draped beside my cheek; her gaze was hard and holding me steady. Above me, her body was rocking slightly, moving as she breathed.

"I'll tell you whatever you want to hear," she said.

I closed my eyes and sensed her voice, soft in the space between us.

"That's what I'm paid to do."

Boxes

She wears red hot-pants with a ring of fur around each hem.
That must make it hard for her to walk, Bruce thinks. Or sit, if
her legs were closed, which they aren't – not completely. They
lean, instead, against two tall stacks of glossy-wrapped packages. Her mouth is open, though it's obvious she's not saying
anything.

"Hello, Bruce."

"David!" Bruce stands, whips his gaze from the girlie calendar splayed on David's desk. This is December 2005.

"I apologize for the delay," David says, shaking Bruce's
clammy hand. "The presentation took longer than I expected,
so…" David curves around his desk toward his new Control
Chair XL4. He wipes his palm along his trousers as he sits. The
chair's cushion sighs.

"So," David says. "You're looking well, Bruce. Things must
be getting easier."

"Easier – yup – all the time, one day at a time, they say."
Bruce nods, arrhythmic.

"Excellent, Bruce." David awakens his laptop, lifting the lid.
The aluminum case reflects the lamplight. "Good Bruce, that's

good – one sec, okay? One…" David activates the email pro-gram. The computer *ding-dongs,* bright.

David checks the subject line: **This morning…**

He reads the message from Marie, then pushes the laptop aside. "So." He smiles valiantly. "So that's good."

Bruce nods again. "Yeah, yup, it's good it's… my youngest son, he keeps telling me to fly down, spend the holidays down south. Go to the beach. Have Christmas there, you know, in the sun, with his wife and her family, too – she's got a big family – but…." Bruce shrugs. He lifts his hands – palms up, elbows bent – mimicking a scale of the old-fashioned kind. The scale sways. "It's the first year and all, but I don't know. I guess I missed the cheap fares, right? Three weeks in advance?" Bruce peers at the calendar, trying to focus on the squares.

"Yeah but, you *must* get a senior's discount, though. At *your* age – "

"Yup, yup…" Bruce's hands collapse into his lap. "Will you be seeing your dad for Christmas?" he asks.

"Yes sir. We'll be bringing him home for the day, unless…"

"Unless?"

"Because it disorients him," David continues. "Which is common, they say. They say they get 'disoriented' if they leave the facility." David air-quotes the word. "Which is weird, you know, because he's not really… *oriented*"– air-quote – "not exactly…" David glances at the photograph of his family (wife, two kids and the chocolate lab named Buddy), taken exactly one year ago, just before Christmas. David himself hasn't changed this past year. But Monica, his daughter: she's changed. Oh yes. This was the year she 'blossomed,' according to Marie. That was the word she used: *blossomed.*

David wasn't sure what to call it other than 'weird.' Blossom, okay, but seeing his daughter like that, with breasts and cleavage and tiny skirts… It was weird! In fact, just that morning – that morning, of all mornings! – the dog had taken a maxi pad out of the garbage in Monica's bathroom. He'd ripped that super-absorbent stuff to shreds, tore it all to pieces, leaving bloodied cotton strewn all over the hallway.

David's balls contract at the memory.

"Well, tell him I said hello," Bruce says.

"I'll certainly do that," David lies. "My dad always said you were the best salesman he ever had. 'Get Bruce in a room,' he always said. 'Get him in a room, get him talking, and you got a deal' – he said that."

Bruce flushes red. "Well, tell him I said hello." Bruce looks out the window, toward the long wires linking the towers on the electrical field. Back when Bruce first started working here, that field was filled with wildflowers. He and David Sr. would come to this very office to celebrate each new deal with a glass of Scotch, toasting each other as the sun shone over the scrub. Those were exciting times, those years. They'd built that company – he and David Sr. – bagging clients, building boxes. The door had always been open to Bruce back then, always open wide, but Bruce hadn't stepped in this office for months – not since that consultant came. It was July, Bruce recalls. He knows because the girl in David's calendar was wearing camouflage that month: a sand-coloured camouflage bikini for the Fourth of July. She was saluting, chest out, shoulders back, hair pulled into a bun. Fireworks exploded in the background.

Bruce remembers when camouflage was green.

"Well…"

An email arrives with a bright *ding-dong* sound.

"One sec there, Bruce. Just gimme…"

David checks the subject line: **Please Read! This is not Spam!**

He knows it's too soon to receive a decision. Even so, he thought that maybe his presentation had been so good – with the multimedia aspect, the interactive aspect – that maybe they'd made a quick decision. His presentation had gone well, he thinks; once that glitch got resolved, it had gone very well. Very well, indeed.

"It'll be fine," Bruce continues. "I'm actually looking forward to some quiet this Christmas. Old movies and… I finally got that – the whaddya…" Bruce's hand circles through the air, as if to churn up the word. "That… the… the DVD player. My neighbour's kid, he said he'd show me how to use it, 'cause… I don't know… I tried it, but I couldn't get it working."

"Right. So that's good, so…"

"It's not the hook-up – that I can do. I can do that. I rebuilt many-a-car in my day, believe you me. A '62 Corvette – that was the best one, just took it apart and…." Bruce's fingers fiddle on the desk, manipulating the imaginary insides under the hood of a vehicle. "The wires are simple, I mean, you can see it – how it all fits together – what connects to what and… but the pictures of those buttons on screens," he says. "I click something and then everything changes. The pictures of the buttons – they just change. Just – "

Bruce's hand bumps into the photo of David's family; David watches him fumble with the frame.

"They just…"

David had been there, months ago, when the consultant

told Bruce that he gesticulated too much. 'Mr. Altman, you look like a mime,' she'd said, right to his face, in front of the staff. She'd folded her arms beneath her breasts. Mimes, she'd continued, do not project confidence and modernity. Mimes, she'd concluded, are annoying.

"I just can't figure out the pictures," Bruce says, putting his hands in his lap. He twirls his wedding band with his thumb. It's still too soon to remove it.

"So Bruce," David starts, adjusting the photo. "It's almost a new year."

"Almost, that's right. It's December after all!"

"Our company's gone through many changes this year."

"That's true, I agree." He nods. He adds, "I love the new sign by the way."

"Do you?" David becomes animated. "I wasn't sure because –"

"Oh no, it's great. It's really… it's classy." He jabs – *classy* – nailing the word to the air between them.

"You think so? Good, 'cause it cost me…" David mutters then recalls himself. "And you should see the new website. It's got all these photos and graphics and those… the pop-up menus, and… Have you seen it?"

"I have… not, no," Bruce says. "My brain just doesn't get it, I guess!" he laughs. "I guess my – "

"But you see, though, Bruce: that's a problem." David's voice gets stiff and square, its edges unassailable. "It's a new world out there."

"It is, no doubt."

"A brave new world."

"No doubt. A brave new world. I agree, undoubtedly."

The new secretary strides through the hallway with a large

stack of files. She passes the girl who sits scribbling in her journal, waiting to collect her cheque. She was all over the website, this girl. She wasn't *really* a model, just a friend of a friend of the photographer. An artist of some sort; they all hang out together, the artists, the creators, the 'creative class.' So she wasn't a model but she was pretty, though. Pretty without being beautiful; pretty like friendly, neighbourly, making you feel confident. Plus, she'd take what they could pay, which wasn't much.

David stares.

The secretary returns. Her stockings are sheer black.

Bruce nods, then speaks into the vacancy. "I was talking to my son – the youngest – about that very thing. It's a new world and it's different, sure – it's *brave* but not 'brave' like the old days. Not like when…"

The old secretary wasn't *nearly* as efficient, David assures himself. Besides, she didn't present the right impression, with those dowdy dresses and ill-applied lipstick, the red creeping up the dry skin above her mouth. It was unseemly.

"Because your father believed – "

She'd cried, though, that old secretary: right here in the office, she'd clung onto David and wept. She didn't see it coming.

Bruce is still talking.

He's gesticulating, saying something about honesty and virility.

Bruce is talking about virility? David tries to pay attention.

"That's great, Bruce," he says. "Very true. But here's the thing…"

The new secretary knocks on the door. She whisper-shouts to David that she needs his signature. "David," she mouths.

"Just gimme one sec there, Bruce," David says, bounding

to the doorway.

Bruce nods. He looks beyond the pair, toward the hall-way where a woman sits, writing beneath the newly mounted, blown-up photo that fully covers the wall. It's a photograph of an aisle in a supermarket, hundreds of products stacked verti-cally, extending horizontally, looming huge then and zooming into oblivion. 'Products by PackSoln' was written across the top:

PRODUCTS BY PACKSOLN

GET YOUR GOODS INTO *THEIR* HANDS

GIVE YOUR GOODS TO PACKSOLN!

Family Owned Since 1964

The supermarket isn't *really* a supermarket, as Bruce is well aware: PackSoln's packages wouldn't fill an aisle of a supermar-ket. Not anymore. Not at this rate.

The photo shoot had been arranged by the consultant.

"That's right!" David laughs.

The woman looks up and catches Bruce's eye. They ponder each other for a while. Bruce recognizes her, vaguely. He as-sociates her with anxiety, though he can't quite imagine why.

"That's right! Computers can't take over yet – who'd sign the cheques?"

She's on the website, Bruce realizes; she's the company's 'smart new look,' though she looks far smarter now, in her jeans and glasses. Bruce bows his head and the woman returns to her journal. She writes something.

"Here you go!" David says. He signs the cheque then lays his hand on the secretary's shoulder. "How did we ever manage without you?" he asks. He squeezes, feeling the shoulder pads on her cropped black jacket. A bolero jacket, it's called. David's wife had bought one in Spain last year. She'd made of point of it: 'I need to find a bolero jacket,' she'd said. He and Marie had walked through all of Madrid, it seemed, embarking on some grand quest, some great journey, as if that jacket could transform her. It got to the point where she'd just purse her lips to say the 'B' – '*bo*-lero jacket' – and they'd start to laugh, just the two of them, the kids getting all angry about it – about the laughing – like it was so odd that their parents would be silly. Or happy maybe.

"Thanks!" David calls again. The secretary winks then motions to the girl who stands, still scribbling. They disappear around the corner.

"So Bruce," David says, returning to his chair. "What was I saying?"

"You were saying…"

"I was saying… What I was saying is…" He pauses. "We need to show our clients that we're… what we are is hip!" he says. "We're not dinosaurs here!"

"God no! We're *hip*, for sure."

"We're so hip we listen to Dylan the second time around!" David slaps his desk. "I tell my son, 'I know that song! I've known for years – decades! I knew it was good *then*, and *why* it was good, and why it's good *now*.'"

"That's right, that's right." Bruce nods, arrhythmic.

Bruce didn't listen to Dylan either time around. But he'd had an affair with a girl who'd worshipped Dylan – a hippy with long hair and no bra and that stupid 'love' smile. It was the one time he'd been unfaithful to Celia – one time in thirty-six years of marriage. He'd told her about it this spring, right at the end, right when they were saying everything.

"I tell him – "

An email comes in, making a *ding-dong* sound, bright. "One sec," David says. He fingers the mouse pad. "See what I mean! We're not dinosaurs! We're…"

Subject: **Final Payment Overdue**

David moves the cursor to the trash icon but doesn't push.

Bruce twirls his ring. Bruce's youngest son had sent an email announcement when Celia died. Bruce was cc'ed, even though he knew, of course. He'd stayed with her in the hospital that entire day. He'd taken off the oxygen mask so they could talk through that final glorious burst of strength. They talked about the kids, the old days, their honeymoon even; they talked about that week on the beach in Jamaica, with her so startlingly beautiful in her bikini and long hair, walking up the sand with a pink conch in her palm. They talked and remembered and never discussed it – her death – though they both knew it was coming. She'd given him a gift, Bruce knows, with the quiet ease of her passing. He'd held her hand for a long time after.

'Some Important News.' That's what their son had titled the email.

David is slumped in his Control Chair. "I guess what I'm saying is… it's… we have to communicate to our clients that we understand their needs."

"Yes."

"We listen to them. We provide solutions."

"Solutions, of course, that's right. We're Pack*Soln* after all."

"We are. And they don't understand how important we

are." David sits up, chest expanding. "If you strip the design, you still have the *package*, the outer *shell*, the *box*."

"The box. The box is *very* important."

"It is…. You see, *you* understand, Bruce," David says. "Most people don't. Even our new sales team – some of them don't… they don't see the box's *construction*. They can't imagine the intricacy of it."

"They don't have the imagination, the – "

"That's it – the imagination! They need to *imagine* how to *construct* this three-dimensional package, this box. They need to conceive the way in to the product – "

"The opening, the access – "

"Do you enter directly through the top? Is the opening obvious or concealed?"

"And don't forget the space around – " Bruce's arms circle.

"The space around the product, of course," David says. "Is there room for the product to move? Or is it tight?"

"And how is it kept in place – or maybe it isn't."

"Maybe it isn't – that's right! But why not?"

"There could be a reason."

"*Many* reasons. Very *good* reasons. But they need to be *thought* about. All of these… all… and the images – the figures – the colour: do you want the package to absorb the ink – dull the ink – or let it pop?"

"Do you want the figures to fold around in three dimensions," Bruce demonstrates, gesticulating, "or remain on one side only?"

"Two dimensions or three – which do you want and *why*. What does that say about the *product*."

"About what's inside."

"Do you know how *important* those boxes are? Do you re-alize what the boxes *say,* even though no one is *aware* of it?"

An email *ding-dongs,* bright. David ignores it.

"I do," Bruce nods. "Your father taught me that, right here in this office, right in this room."

"Right! Yes! In this..." David continues, chin up, looking toward the photo in the hallway. "Because *advertising* they no-tice. *Advertising* they teach. Kids get 'Media Studies' in high school, for God's sake." He quotes with his fingers: 'Media Studies.' "My son – his friends – they all know how to take apart ads but they love 'em anyway, don't they," David grunts. "They fall for it anyway, like it's some great rebellion to fall for it anyway, even though they *know* they're being had, they *know* they're being..."

"They're being..." Bruce gesticulates for the word.

"That's right! But no one notices the *packages.* The *boxes.* No one notices that."

A *ding-dong* sound announces the arrival of an email. "One sec," David says, somewhat flushed.

Bruce looks at the photo of David's family. My God, he thinks, David has gotten old....

David is reading the email. His hand grabs his mouth, his whole hand there on his face. "They just don't understand how important we are," he mutters, his voice smothered.

Bruce watches David. He hears the new secretary tinkle-laugh in the hallway. The girl is watching them, though she's stopped taking notes. She has her cheque; she's watching them.

Bruce notices the snow outside the window, falling on the sparse electrical fields. He scratches his head. "Anything important?" he asks. Some of his scaly-dried scalp lodges beneath his fingernails.

"They just don't bloody understand."

Bruce flicks the scum from under his nail. "That's because we're dinosaurs, David," he says.

David shuts his laptop with a conclusive click. "You've been doing this for a long time, haven't you," he says.

"I have."

David peers at the calendar, as if it could show him all those thirty-odd years. "That thing has got to go," he says, pointing to the calendar. "Our consultant insists on it."

"Is that so? She insists?"

David guffaws. "She told me to get rid of it this summer but I was trying to hold on – to keep a few things like they were. I was trying, but..."

"But it's a new world out there. You said so yourself, David. Email, the web – there's no more face-to-face..." Bruce hand glides through the air, passing from David to himself. "No more conversation or – "

"No."

" – just smiley-faced emails with those – whaddya – the punctuation marks."

"I hate those goddamn smiley faces."

"They're pretty stupid, aren't they."

"I hate email."

Bruce chuckles. "I should probably learn to use it better," he says.

"Don't bother."

Bruce does not respond.

David looks up. "I – "

"It's okay, David," Bruce says. He holds out his palm, flat

and firm: *Stop*, it says. "It's okay. I see what you mean."

"It's not – I'm not…"

"It's okay. Really. I need a rest anyway."

David sighs, stares at the open lips of Miss Klaus, that empty open mouth. "My dad always said you were the best salesman he ever had."

"Those were different times…." Bruce stands, extends his hand across the desk. David takes it; he holds onto that moist warmth, unwilling to let go.

"I don't know what to say. I don't know how…"

"How 'bout this," Bruce says. "I'll check my email this weekend, okay David? Just… I'll definitely come to the office and check my email. That's all I'm saying."

"Thank you, Bruce. Thanks for…"

"Yup, yeah. Just tell your dad I said hello, okay?" Bruce slips his hand away and walks out the office door. David watches him pass through the hallway; he pauses to greet the girl, who's tucking her cheque in her journal. Bruce does not gesticulate. The girl looks at his eyes, then his hands.

As the two leave the building, David opens his laptop. He reads the subjects stacked:

Today's Proposal…

Change Your Life!

Final Payment Overdue

Please Read! This is not Spam!

This morning…

David hits the 'new' icon. He begins to type.

Subject: **Thank You For Your Years of Service**

He sits with his fingers on the keys, watching the single vertical line pulse on the big, grey box where he's supposed to write his message. He stares. The computer *ding-dongs,* bright.

Subject: **Where are you? I'm going out**

Without responding to his wife, David returns to his main message. He maneuvers the cursor to the appropriate spot on the screen. He clicks once and goes home, where the dog will greet him with darting, happy licks across his face and mouth.

Layers

Red ants and rain; stained skin and rough hands; a man's voice, a woman's moan. These are my memories of that day. They wouldn't become a story for twenty-five years.

MAY 2007.
18 GRENADIER ROAD, TORONTO.
ON THE PHONE TO GARDEN CITY, NEW YORK.

"He was such a shit," she says.

That conversation leads back, then, into this: the memory I'd recalled, on occasion, over the course of three decades.

"It's more complicated than that," I say.

It wasn't a coherent memory – not exactly. It was more a series of dense sensations, feelings whose meaning I wouldn't grasp until I was older.

"Perhaps," my mother replies.

My mother: she is the one who controlled the facts. She revealed them to me at certain, specific moments in our relationship. These moments, with her, traversed my memory of that day, animating the elements.

"It's always more complicated, mom."

And that's how it all came together: confusions and questions, sensations remembered in physical detail, a fact strategically disclosed – *this* is how I come to know the story in its fullness.

MARCH 1989.
71 THIRD STREET, GARDEN CITY, NEW YORK.
IN THE BREAKFAST ROOM.

"Hey – did you hear me? I said I'll be back by dinner.... Hey!"

She pokes me.

"What."

"I'll be back by dinner," she repeats.

"Fine," I say limply.

"Fine," she rejoins.

She hovers beside the couch where I lie, reading a novel. The cushions are askew. I turn the page.

"Okay..." She gulps a glass of water. I can hear the clunk in her throat as the liquid goes down. It disgusts me.

"I'll be back by dinner but I probably won't be hungry. They always serve food at these functions, although nobody ever eats. Who wants to eat after seeing that? Huh?... Marianne?"

"I wouldn't know," I say, aware of the bulge beside me, where I've hidden bread and muffins beneath the cushions. I will binge-and-purge as soon as my mother leaves.

"Huh? Marianne?"

She shoves and I look up. Her eyes seem misshapen, the lids peeled back from her raging emotion – either anger or anxiety, I'm not sure which. Not that it matters with her. Anger, anxiety: one becomes the other becomes the cause of a fight between us. I am sixteen years old. She doesn't have a job, except to raise me. I have an eating disorder that we don't discuss.

"Sure," I say. "Fine."

"Fine. Well," she says, shifting her balance. "Well, I'll be back by dinner, regardless. The internment should be done by three."

"The what?"

"The internment," she says. "The burial? Do you remember Mr. Fischer?"

"Who?"

"Elizabeth's father."

Yes.

"He died?"

"He did," she says. "Another one dead of cancer. And he was so young." She snaps her purse open and shut, removing a handkerchief. "But you wouldn't remember him, from that weekend we went up there. That day – it wasn't even a weekend, it was just a day... but what a day... but you wouldn't remember it," she says. "You were just a kid."

I remember.

She talks about how young he was, Mr. Fischer, a social worker at the Y M C A in Manhattan – in Harlem, no less – an extraordinary man, she says. As she talks I stare at the book, pretending to read. But the story I construct is the memory of that day: he put his hand on my back as I crouched on the stone; my arms were wrapped around my knees. I was listening to the argument while watching the ants. The stick was wet in my hand. I gasped.

It hurts, doesn't it, he said. He stood in the doorway.

It does, I whispered.

It stops, he responded.

The sting on my calf swelled.

He came to me then, put his hand on my back. It's okay, he said. He pulled me to him, scooped me onto his lap. I remained in a ball. It's okay, he repeated. It's okay, my sweet girl, it's okay. He kissed my hair. I felt his voice, a soft-edged vibration that took away the shrill sound of the woman's scream. It's okay.

I looked through the window, into the kitchen where the women stood. The kettle was spewing a cloud of steam; it parted, disturbed, as my mother stepped toward her friend, who was trembling.

"And Elizabeth is devastated, just devastated." My mother starts to cry. "He was such a good man. Such a good father. He never judged Elizabeth – never once, and she told him *everything*. Always, he was there for her – even at the very worst of times, he was there – and now Elizabeth has no one. No one!" My mother reaches blindly through her tears to hug me. She clutches at my arms, leaning onto the cushion that conceals the hidden food.

I stiffen.

I tell her that the snot is going to fuck up her makeup if she keeps crying.

My sweet girl, he said. I nuzzled into his chest. My sweet girl, it's okay.

MARCH 1995.

1000 FIFTH AVENUE, NEW YORK CITY.

METROPOLITAN MUSEUM OF ART, AMERICAN WING.

I follow her through unfamiliar empty rooms, past smoothbosomed goddesses and the sloppy hearts of Jim Dine. With every gallery we enter, my mother flashes her badge and I examine a poster – yet another poster – for the retrospective of Dali.

"This wing is closed to the public today," she says as she strides past a guard. "It'll be nice and quiet."

She's been working as a docent for the past five years, ever since I left home to attend university. I've now signed the contract for my first book, a memoir about eating disorders. This is to be our celebratory afternoon.

"How will Elizabeth find us?" I ask, trailing behind my mother. "If this wing is closed…"

"Elizabeth can't come," my mother replies.

"But – !"

"What?"

"But this whole thing was her idea!"

"Well, she's been detained by a work emergency," my mother says and strides by the Tiffany windows. She does not pause to admire these scintillating scenes; she knows they are too primly lovely for me. She turns into the next gallery.

"Some of this stuff is dull," my mother declares. She gestures toward the huge canvas of Washington crossing the white-frothed Delaware. "Very heroic. Mythic even – historic – but *I* like it because *I'm* an historian."

"Right," I say.

"Let's continue."

My mother is not really a historian. She had *intended* to be a historian; she went to Harvard to *become* a historian. But she quit after her master's degree, then taught history in high school in a rich suburban town, then got pregnant. Then she

69

stopped completely. Harvard is where she met Elizabeth.

"So Elizabeth can't meet us at all?" I ask. "I don't get it: what's the 'work emergency'?"

"I don't know, Marianne, she didn't say. She needs to be discreet, of course."

Of course, discretion is part of her job: a therapist can't discuss her clients' problems. And Elizabeth is a wonderful therapist, my mother asserts. Even in their casual conversations, Elizabeth can isolate and articulate the emotional underpinnings of people's behavior: what they need from each other, how those needs warp what they say and do, why they 'choose' what they need in the first place.... My mother puts choice in air-quotes – 'choose' what they need – then adjusts the cheap metal chain that holds her docent badge. Her red-painted nails click against the plastic that laminates her name: *Frances Apostolides*. "Although…"

My mother stops in front of a large canvas.

"Although," she repeats, "she can't seem to understand the people in her own life. Her personal life," she clarifies. "Her *intimate* life, such as it is."

I don't ask her to explain.

My chest, I felt, was breathing too fast.

Fran, I don't know what to do.... What do I do – *Fran!* – what do I *do!* She screamed a second time. My belly felt heavy, a warmth like pee except not that.

What do I *do!*

I picked up a stick and poked at the mound of beige earth between the patio's stones. A clump of dirt landed on a wet leaf. They appeared, then, an instant swarm: red ants with neon, turgid bodies. I watched them crawl all over each other

– legs on torsos on heads, all moving in random writhe, these disgusting red creatures. I stared at them.

If I heard his voice, she said. If I could talk to him, he'd explain – I know he would, I know him, he could explain…. He *could!* I need to *talk* to him. Get a-*way* from me dad! I heard the shove, the toppled objects. Get away!

Elizabeth…

Get a-*way!*

The ants were probing my toes. I watched them, feeling a warm prickling on the back of my neck. I hugged my knees tighter, curling my spine and clenching the muscles.

Don't worry, Mr. Fischer, my mother said. Go ahead, go outside. I've got this here.

But maybe I should –

Please, Mr. Fischer. Just go outside for a while.

A drop of sweat ran down my neck, beneath my hair. The ants were mounting my foot.

Careful, he said. His voice was dry. Careful, Marianne: they bite.

Ants can't bite, I whispered. I watched them crawling over my skin. I gasped.

It hurts, doesn't it….

It does.

It stops, he responded. Eventually, it will stop.

"Now this," my mother says, "I love." She's admiring *Madame X* by John Singer Sargent. The woman's skin is pale. Her fingers are poised on the dark wood table; she peers haughtily over her shoulder. "This caused quite a scandal." My mother describes the history of the portrait: the artist in Paris, seducing the socialite who posed for him, her shoulders bare, the black dress dipped low between her breasts. She explains that Sargent was forced to add dress-straps into the final version of the painting.

"I didn't know that story," I say. It's there, though, in the canvas itself: *Madame X* is not the passive object of the painter's gaze; instead, she's a potent force in the relationship between them. Capture me, she says in his strokes. Try. I will let you try.

I see that now.

"She's beautiful," I say.

I look to my side, to my mother, who is in profile.

She sighs and eases her stance. "Elizabeth really wanted to be here," she says. "But she got that emergency call…. She needed to take it, I guess," She turns to me.

"It's okay," I say. I shrug. It's okay.

My mother reaches to touch my hair but I step aside, pretending ignorance of this attempt. She scratches her neck, then suggests we check out the retrospective. I agree.

MARCH 2000.
129 CHESTNUT AVENUE, TORONTO.
IN THE LIVING ROOM.

The couch smells sour. Some of my milk has squirted onto the cushions and I haven't found the time to wash it off. My husband is working ten hours a day – ten hours he's up there, at his 'home office,' working for various clients. He's got a big deal 'on-the-go.' I heard him discuss the details with my dad while I scrubbed the dishes stacked in the sink. At least his depression seems abated. My daughter fusses; I unstrap my maternity bra.

"Does she eat, like, every hour?" my mother asks. She sits on a chair across from me. This is her first grandchild.

"Whenever she's hungry," I reply.

"When you were a kid, we were told to put you on a schedule. Just let you cry and cry – my God, you had strong lungs! And three hours after the last feeding, *then* we could feed you," she says. "With a bottle, of course. Because at that time they told us – and what did we know, we just listened to the doctors at that time because, back then, of course...

She talks into her nervousness, like always. I get my child into position.

"...I would've breastfed you, but they told us not to," she says. She peers at my breast, which is bigger than my daughter's head. "I wouldn't have let you cry like that if it was my choice. Believe me," she adds. "It was *hard* on me. It was *hard* to listen to you cry but

I seethe, breathing in as my daughter drinks. The blood blisters are unspeakably painful. They dot my nipples like a contagion: florid, pin-prick bumps that seem to glow on the pale, pink tissue. These were made by the power of my baby's suck; they will soon dry up and fall off, the midwife assures me.

"...did we know! It's interesting to think what you'd do differently, in retrospect, if you had a choice. 'If I knew then what I know now!'" She forces a laugh out her mouth.

I ignore her and stroke the slick, womb-soft hair on my daughter's scalp. My nipple throbs.

My mother is silent.

She pours herself some water from a hand-thrown clay pitcher, a wedding gift from my husband's friend – a poet who could ill-afford that finely-shaped, curve-lipped object. He was always extravagant, that poet.

She drinks. She is quiet. We listen to the desperate, panting sounds of my daughter as she takes the milk. My mother pours herself more water.

"Elizabeth Fischer was jealous of me," she says, more softly now. "When I had you, a little girl... Do you remember Elizabeth?"

"Of course I remember. We saw her a few years ago – or, almost ... in the museum? When we saw that painting –"

"Right – when we saw the Dali exhibit – of course ... well, she always said you were like her own," my mother continues. "She always wanted to have kids."

"Oh," I say, confused. "I thought she chose to be a career woman."

"Hardly," my mother says. "It was the greatest disappointment in her life, not having kids." She combs her hair with her fingers, exposing the grey roots. "It was a great disappointment, I should say." She nods, confirming the correction.

They were hugging before I'd unbuckled the belt. They didn't notice me when I stepped from the car, onto the gravel driveway. I stood awkwardly, waiting. I scratched at my scalp through the layers of hair, which was pulled back into a ponytail, frizzed from the rain. A man stood in the doorway. Look at you, all grown up, he said. The women were talking as they hugged; their words sounded like moans. Do you remember me? I met you when you were just a baby.

"You are lucky to have a daughter."

Can I brush your hair? Elizabeth asked. There was such longing in her voice – such naked need – that I could not but say yes.

Yes.

The man was no longer in the doorway.

I stood by the car which was warm, almost steaming. I looked down; the driveway was strewn with quashed pink petals, a torrent brought down by the storm. The bushes were overgrown.

I'm too late, she said. I bet it was beautiful here two weeks ago.

It's beautiful here now, my mother replied. She touched her friend's arm with tender assurance.

No, Fran… No, it's too late.

The man stepped outside again. He held a hairbrush clogged with strands of brown and grey.

Thank you dad, she said.

I slid the elastic down my ponytail. My hair felt too heavy in the humid air.

That's nice, she said. She started at the roots instead of the ends. She spoke on occasion, whispering to me. It's a bit tangly here. Are you okay? Does it hurt too much? She put her hand on my shoulder as if she were protecting me. Are you okay, Marianne?

Yes, I acquiesced. I tried to keep my muscles stiff so my head didn't jerk back: she was tugging too hard, unpracticed at brushing a young girl's hair.

I'm so glad you're here, he said to my mother. Elizabeth needs a friend right now. I can only do so much….

Yes.

You have beautiful hair.

Thank you.

You are a beautiful girl.

Thank you.

Hair gets coarse as you get older. It changes, she said. She brushed. A little girl's hair is quite special.

My eyes are watering from the pain.

"You are a beautiful girl."

MARCH 2005.

333 RONCESVALLES AVENUE, TORONTO.

ALTERNATIVE GROUNDS CAFÉ.

I pour my fourth cup of coffee. It won't help, I realize; nothing will give back those midnight hours when I should've been sleeping. I sip the drink, harsh and black.

"Read me a book," my daughter demands.

"In a minute," I say. I rub my eyes. "Just let me have this coffee, okay?"

My daughter starts to whine.

"Were you out late last night?" my mother asks. She's in town for my daughter's fifth birthday. My son is asleep in the stroller.

"Late? What? Yeah… The reading took longer than usual. There were three poets and some of us – a *bunch* of us – went out after, so…"

"Mommy!"

"*I'll* read you the book," my mother says, patting her lap. My daughter climbs up. "Let's let your mommy rest. She's working very hard."

"Thank you," I say.

"It's true, Marianne. You're pursuing your dream. I wish *I'd* had the courage to do that," she adds. "I'm very proud of you."

I slump, sweating; my skin smells of scotch and night-sheets. "Don't be," I say.

"Cinderella," she begins.

I go to the counter and ask for a glass of water. I chat with a pregnant mother, who describes her son's nap schedule; surprisingly, her cervix is already dilating. She tells me this is normal. She chases her son.

By the time I walk back to the table, Cinderella is attending the third ball. She is headed for trouble – the clock striking twelve, the breathless rush home, the glass shoe lost – then the story will resolve in marriage. The book will end and my daughter will be satisfied. I drink my coffee. She twirls her hair, looking intently at the pictures, surrounded by the romance of this tale.

"Elizabeth Fischer is getting married," my mother says, interrupting the book.

"You're kidding – she's almost seventy, isn't she?"

"Keep reading!"

"One second, sweetheart."

"He's a nice man. They'll take care of each other."

"Ah – the eternal passion of marriage," I say.

My mother stares, silent for a moment. "She might have wanted passion at one point," she says, "but she wants something different now."

I close my eyes; the words have injured.

"I'm sorry," I say.

"Keep reading!"

"I'm sorry."

He was rocking me, rhythmic. I was curled in his lap.

Let's have a snack, my mother said, carrying a tray to the

patio. Some tea and strawberries.

Strawberries, Elizabeth said. I was going to feed him strawberries… fresh strawberries. She took one from the bowl.

"He raised the slipper."

He lifted me to standing, his hands large around my ribs; he stood.

I thought that would be very romantic.

He doesn't deserve it, my mother said. He doesn't…

I shoved the berries into my mouth: three, then four. They were large and cool, sliding against my cheeks.

He does, she insisted.

"He called after her."

You don't deserve this, my mother said. *You* don't.

He's not coming, is he….

I swallowed the fruit, squeezing it down my throat. I grabbed more berries from the bowl; their juice made a dark line beneath my nails, where the skin attached.

"The prince knocked on the door. On the royal pillow was a single glass slipper."

"Mommy, where did you get those shoes?" my daughter asks. "The ones you wore last night? Those were pretty. Did daddy give you those?"

"No," I say, "he didn't give me the shoes."

"Did he give you the necklace?… Or the earrings?…"

My mother sets the book aside.

"I liked those earrings, mommy. Did he give you those?" My daughter's voice is upward-inflected, filled with the bright near-innocence of childhood. "Daddy gave you those, right mommy?"

"No, baby," I respond. "He only gave me the ring."

It's time to go, Marianne. We should go now.... My mother stepped toward me. She took my hand, which was reaching into the berry bowl.

Daddy?

Elizabeth's father spread his arms wide. I watched her fall into him, her coarse hair covering her face. He held her. He kissed her scalp.

It's okay, he said. The ants scurried around their feet.

Is it over, daddy?

My sweet girl...

It's over, isn't it....

She looked up, into his face.

He paused.

Please tell me....

Yes baby, he said. It's over.

Her body heaved. I watched them sway as I waved good-bye. They did not see me.

"And the glass slipper slid perfectly onto her delicate foot."

"Hooray!" my daughter says.

I get up and go to the bathroom. I try to remember when my period is due.

MAY 2007.

18 GRENADIER ROAD, TORONTO.

ON THE PHONE TO GARDEN CITY, NEW YORK.

I sit on the bed by the open window, the hem of my brief, cotton robe draped across my thighs. I stare at the phone, whose display counts the duration of the call: ten minutes and twenty-one seconds. Twenty-two. It is a Saturday night and I'm alone in my apartment, talking with my mom. I'm lonely.

I tell her this.

"It's lonely, mom."

My daughter's plastic princess is lying on my bed. She and her brother are gone, with their dad. I won't see them for a week.

My mother urges me to watch a movie – something mindless, she says. I don't respond. She continues to make suggestions; she recounts, blow-by-blow, the plot of a 'mindless' movie she recently saw – a movie that obviously engaged her mind because she still remembers every scene, it seems, because she's still talking. My mother knows she's doing the wrong thing. She pauses. "I wish I were there to help," she says. "To give you a hug or something."

"A hug would be good," I say. It's been months since I was hugged or touched by any adult – casually, lovingly, sexually or otherwise. The affair didn't last the separation.

"It's been such a hard year for you," my mother says. "I wish I could hop in the car right now, just drive up and give you a hug."

I say nothing.

"I did that for someone once…."

"I remember."

My mother never drove in the rain and yet I was hustled into that car. She put her key in the ignition and unfolded a map. She exhaled. Let's do this, she said to herself. Rhode Island. She turned on the all-news radio station with its 'traffic and weather together' every fifteen minutes. We were driving into the storm, but we didn't need the radio to tell us that: from the passenger's seat, I could see the dark clouds moving over each other, becoming more palpably dense.

Let's do this.

She was unusually calm. I took her lead: I did not argue with her; this was bigger than me.

Where are we going, I asked.

"I wouldn't have driven," she says. "You know how I hate to drive in the rain."

"I do –"

"But I got that phone call…. She was screaming," she says. "I didn't know what was happening. It was terrible."

"But why –"

"He was supposed to meet her that weekend. He was supposed to leave his wife…"

"Who's 'he'?"

"…and meet her there, at her father's summer house on Rhode Island. It was all set up."

"But who –"

"Her lover."

I smile sadly in the slow spread of understanding. I look through my apartment. It is bare of beautiful objects, all of which I left with him, my ex-husband, in his house that used to be ours. All except the lovely pitcher, which he didn't want.

"I didn't know," I say.

Elizabeth said their love couldn't be illicit anymore. They'd been together for two years – meeting in hotel rooms, fucking in cars, her mouth on his, on him, his words. He'd said I love you. He'd said he'd leave his wife.

Meet me at the house, she'd asserted, finally. Meet me there. Meet my father. Make this more than a fantasy.

"I didn't know she'd had an affair," I repeat.

Make this real.

He'd said yes.

He was supposed to arrive at the house on Saturday. On Tuesday, Elizabeth called my mother.

"Can you imagine? Three days of waiting in that house? Afraid to leave in case he showed up? And she couldn't talk to her dad about it…. She wasn't ready to talk to him, even though they shared everything. Can you imagine the disappointment? The humiliation?"

"Affairs get complicated," I say and play with the thin, white belt of my robe.

"Well, it wasn't complicated for him," she says. "He never even called!"

"Well –"

"He was such a shit," she declares.

"It's more complicated than that."

"Perhaps."

"It's always more complicated, mom."

Two Dialogues: On Bravery

I flick on the radio, enraged by my lack of progress. I pace in the kitchen, wondering whether to make myself more coffee and get back to work. As I pause in my pacing, arms crossed, I attune to the voice on the radio.

Another soldier has been killed in Afghanistan, we're told. We learn why he joined the army, how he was killed, and the number of children he leaves behind; I listen to the twenty-one gun salute, the sound of the bugle and crying. After a time, the announcer concludes that this "brave soldier" made the "ultimate sacrifice" fighting for "democracy and justice."

I don't have a clue what that means.

I shut off the radio and return to my desk. I stare at the paper. It is filled with scribbles and slashes, marks of my frustration. I can't make the words come out right because I don't understand what I want to say.

I pick up my pen and write these words: "My father is a coward."

৵

Did you understand that your dad could die?

Yeah, you had that sense…. But you also had the sense that *you* could die. Because death was around. It was part of the day.

What do you mean?

When you played, you were conscious of what was around you. Was there a patrol coming by? If there was, you disappeared. If there was an air raid, you ran. 'Cause – as a kid – you know you should run, you should fade. You know instinctively how to do what you *have* to do to protect yourself. But you don't sit and *think* about it. You don't *philosophize* about it. You just *do* it.

You just run.

Right: you run…. But then,

of course, [Dimitri] Laspiti
came and told my parents
what the Communists were
saying.

Which was…

Which was that they considered my father an anti-Com-
munist, and that 'something'
has to be done about it.
And of course, mom was
telling my father a lot, 'Don't
go to the villages.' I remember that: 'Why do you have
to go? They've made the decision to kill you. Don't go.'
And he said, 'Hey, I'm
helping these people. Why
should they want to harm
me?'
I *remember* the conversations. She was literally on
her hands and knees – *'Don't
go! Don't go!'* – begging him.

But he went.

Of course he went.

Does that make you angry with
your father – that he didn't
heed the warnings?

No, not at all. No. He wasn't

the kind of person to live in
fear.

∽

Plato undertakes the first philosophical examination of bravery in his early Socratic dialogue, "Laches." Within this work, he questions the meaning of bravery: how do we define and understand that concept? How can it be taught, or brought into one's possession?

One of Socrates' interlocutors, the celebrated General Laches, argues that bravery is defined by a man's actions. "If a man is prepared to stand in the ranks, face up to the enemy and not run away, you can be sure that he is brave," he states.

Socrates dismisses that definition as overly specific.

The concept – bravery – must apply to public *and* private life, to situations as diverse as battlefield engagements and sexual temptations. "I wanted to find out," Socrates clarifies, "what it is to be brave in the face of an illness, in the face of poverty, and in public life." In other words, bravery doesn't concern only "resisting pain or fear" but also "putting up stern opposition to temptation and indulgence."

Laches readily agrees; guided by Socrates, he offers a revised definition. Bravery is "a certain endurance present in one's character" – an endurance "accompanied by wisdom."

Laches seems satisfied with this definition.

The reader seems satisfied, too.

The satisfaction doesn't last long.

In a dizzying interaction – one that focuses on a battlefield scenario – Socrates leads Laches to state the *opposite* of his initial belief. Laches is flummoxed, surprised by the words his mouth has been made to speak; it's as if a hand has reached inside his throat, contorted his voice to form a conclusion he didn't intend.

Like so many of Socrates' interlocutors, Laches now gives up, completely muddled.

Into this breach steps Nicias, another celebrated general.

Celebrated, cocky and competitive.

Bravery, Nicias asserts, doesn't concern action or character. The essential element of bravery is knowledge, specifically "knowledge of what is fearful and what is encouraging, both in wartime and in all other situations."

Since *knowledge* is the basis of bravery, children and animals can never be brave. They may be "fearless" or "unafraid," but not "brave." A child's lack of fear, Nicias explains, arises from an inability to anticipate the consequences of his action or inaction. "Bravery and foresight are, in my opinion, things a very small number of people possess; whereas being reckless, daring, fearless and blind to consequences is the norm for the vast majority of men, women, children and animals."

With a new definition now proposed, Socrates begins to question Nicias.

Once again, he alters the surface of the argument – the words themselves – by entering the argument's interior logic. Here, the stumbling point regards the nature of time.

Bravery – "knowledge of what is fearful and encouraging" – exclusively concerns the *future* in Nicias' argument. However, Nicias' logic doesn't adequately isolate the future from the past and the present. All three phases of time are linked: "It's never one thing to know how a past event took place, another to know how events are unfolding in the present, and another to know how future events will come about and what the best course for them would be: it's the same knowledge throughout," says Socrates.

Nicias agrees.

Therefore, Socrates continues, Nicias has failed to distinguish bravery from another basic concept: namely goodness. "What you're doing now, Nicias, won't be a *part* of goodness, but goodness in its entirety."

"So it seems," agrees Nicias.

"But we did say that bravery is only *one* of the parts of goodness."

"Yes, we did."

"But what you're now describing appears not to be so."

"No, it seems not."

"So we've *not* discovered what bravery is, Nicias."

"No, apparently not."

When Nicias speaks his own failure – brought there by Socrates – he doesn't get flummoxed, he gets vexed. Instead of contemplating this reversal of logic, he picks a fight with Laches. "That's marvelous, Laches, I must say!" Nicias spews. "A minute ago you were shown to know nothing at all about bravery, and now you don't think it matters anymore: so long as I'm shown up in the same light, that's all that bothers you. We're both totally ignorant of things any self-respecting man ought to know, but apparently it won't make any difference to you now! It strikes me you're behaving in a typically human way – you keep an eye on others, but you never take a good look at yourself."

On this note, the men part company, never arriving at any adequate definition of bravery.

TAPE #12, SIDE A.
Continued.

Do you know who was responsible for killing your father?

As far as names? There
were names that were
floated around. But no, I
never learned who the killer
was…. I never learned what
happened to that man – if
he was punished, or… I
should've learned.

How would you have done
that?

You'd make it a mission in
your life.

Do you think that's a worthy
mission?

The question is: What would
it have done for *me*. Would
it have been cathartic or not.

What's 'it'?

Revenge.

Revenge?! Like, tracking him
down and seeking some form
of vengeance?

I mean, you're not gonna go

89

and *kill* someone….

What would you have done
then? Imagine….

I have no idea. It's finding
out. And getting to the point
where you have an option.

But –

And I don't *know* what I'd
do at that point. If I was in
Greece and got caught up
with this?… [Long pause.]
Yeah, I could probably end
up getting retribution.

[Accusative silence.]

I don't *know,* Marianne! I
don't *know* what's in me!
Anger? Yes. The sense of
revenge? Maybe, maybe… I
don't know….

So what happens to that anger?

It was totally suppressed –
totally suppressed – until
you started asking questions.

Well, it couldn't have gone
nowhere.

For thirty, forty years I
didn't think about it. Period.
But it *did* affect me…. And
then, of course, it leaves
doubts about yourself.

What do you mean, 'doubts about yourself'?

Do I have it in me to do that? Or am I just a coward.

༄

What's fascinating about the early Socratic dialogues – and what Laches and Nicias don't realize – is that Socrates isn't dismissing his interlocutors' *conclusions*, only their *logic*. Through his questioning, Socrates excavates the argument. He doesn't probe and poke. Instead, he eats – he asks – from within the assumptions and causal relationships that constitute the argument itself. In doing so, he shows that the structure of the logic is wrong. Not the *surface* of the argument – its conclusion and content – but the *structure*.

༄

TAPE #12, SIDE A.
Continued.

Okay, but there's a judgment implicit in that statement. There's a judgment that being able to kill someone is a positive thing.

No, no. The judgment is: Do I have the *guts* to explore it, the guts to explore it.

91

What kind of 'guts' does it take to explore it?

It's a conscious decision. It's an effort. Do I want to know the specifics. Do I want to know who he was. And if I do, then what do I do with that knowledge.

Right. What would you do?

No. The first question comes first. Do I want to know. Do I have the gumption, the strength. Otherwise, you're suppressing it – you're not doing anything – you're modifying it in your own thoughts.

Okay, but I'm still… You're not going to kill someone: You said that. So what's the point of 'making it a mission' to know who the killers were?

It's more for me.

What do you mean.

I would feel that I have done a duty. I: have: done. I haven't lived in fear myself.

୧୨

Question and answer: logic and language. We want to partake. I want the chance to respond – to please the mentor, to prove myself a worthy interlocutor.

Imagine: What does it take to explore it.

Socrates understood this desire. His method, as portrayed in Plato's dialogues, solicits our involvement. By the dialogues' very structure, we are asked to raise ourselves to the task of thinking. In other words, "Laches" doesn't teach us what bravery is, but what *thinking* about bravery it.

As we read the dialogue, we try to answer Socrates' questions in our own minds. We displace the failing interlocutor, whether Laches or Nicias; we fantasize that we could satisfy Socrates with the alacrity and depth of our own thinking.

This fantasy is temporary, of course, assuming we've learned anything from the dialogue: Socrates would never allow himself to sit so easily inside any answer. And so we question ourselves more.

ℭℴ

TAPE #28, SIDE A.
TRANSCRIPT PAGES 263-268.
THESSALONIKI, GREECE. JUNE 2002.
Immediately following a visit to the village where Agamemnon Apostolides, my grandfather, was abducted and hanged.

Are you glad you went?

Well, I found out a lot of stuff.

Like…

What's amazing is, you know, the esteem that they had for my father.

Yeah, I saw that.

And through him – *through* him – to me. Because I didn't do anything.

A while ago, when I was planning the trip, you said, 'I'm nervous about going back to the village, because I haven't done anything to avenge my father's death.' Did you feel that when you were there?

Yeah I did – I did. Particularly when I asked, 'Is the killer still around.' And at that moment, I didn't *know* why I wanted to know specifically if that guy's alive or not. But when she [Constantia Laspiti] said, 'He's dead,' that was something different in me than if she'd said, 'He's still alive.' You know, 'He's still alive, he's living the good life.' Then, you know…

Then what.

I don't know 'then what.'

Then what... You wanna
squeeze his balls and make
him scream and yell and say
why he did what he did, or –
what do you want to do...?
Yeah, I'd probably like to do
that.

ॐ

My father spoke at night, exhausted; we'd spent the afternoon
with Constantia Laspiti, the wife of Agamemnon's closest ally
in the villages. Now aged 82, Constantia recalled the day of
Agamemnon's death; she shared some facts and rumours, not
distinguishing between the two. As we sat on her veranda
shaded by olive trees, my father asked very few questions. This
was his first trip to Greece since 1949, the year he immigrated
to the United States. The trip was prompted by my probing,
my unrelenting need to hear his past – to take his stories into
me so I could understand.

ॐ

TAPE #28, SIDE A.
Continued.

> But how do you – my God, that
> must be an odd thing to notice
> about yourself.

What.

> That violent streak.

Mmmm… [His jaw is clenched; the pause is long.] Maybe it's been pent up in there all my life.

Does it frighten you to know that you feel that way? Does it make you feel powerful?

[Guffaw.]

Does it surprise you?

It *does* surprise you because, as I said, I suppressed it. Had I not suppressed it, you know… Because I didn't live with an *anger*, I lived with a *void*.

And the void was…

The void was *avoiding* and not accepting what your life *was* until that point. You know, that's what my life was. You have to face it, you have to live with it, you have to make amends for it. You have to – and I hadn't done that. Period. I hadn't done that. I just ran away from it. I suppressed it.

But –

But it hadn't gone away. It's still there.

96

Okay. But do you think 'dealing with it' would've meant seeking revenge?

Probably.

You don't think it would've meant coming to terms with your grief?

No, you'd *have* to confront that man. You'd have to confront him. If I found that guy living in the suburbs of Athens – hey…. [He jabs with his chin.] It's like, you and your family have suffered and he's rocking his granddaughter on his knee? Huh… No… That ain't sitting too good.

But he's not alive. So it's too late.

Yeah, it's too late. Yes.

☙

'My father is not a coward.'

I put these words on the paper. Within them, I read the petulant assertion of a girl – a daughter who needs her father to be law and honour, truth and justice, especially now that she senses the contours of his story, the ambiguities inherent in history.

I don't know *what's in me.*
Does it frighten you?

My words don't yet constitute the defensible argument of a worthy interlocutor. But they will: they must. I will strengthen them through impeccable logic. I am determined to do so. I will question myself since I lack someone to question me; I will enter my argument from its inside, its muscle and blood, this body: 'My father is not a coward.'

My father is not a coward.

☙

TAPE #28, SIDE A.
Continued.

But what would violence achieve?

Catharsis, period.

And that's the only way to achieve catharsis?

I don't know. I'll have to see. I don't know. But it's *here.* [He bangs on the table.] Not in the U.S.A. It's here.

So when you go back to the U.S., you think it'll just fade again and you'll go back to –

Well, you know, I'll probably suppress it again – get involved in my flowers and

my sailing, my digging in
the garden and working in
the church, and I'll probably
forget about all this.

Do you want to forget about it?

I think I'm better off forget-
ting about it.

Do you think it'll really go
away? Or will it just go back
into its little box?

Probably it'll go back into its
box. I mean, I've lived my
whole life with it, some-
how…. But this was not
cathartic at all.

It just stirred things up.

Hm?… Yeah.

It left things unresolved.

It's unresolved, yeah.

It's always been unresolved, but
now –

But now it has *surfaced* again.

It's in front of your face.

[He purses his lips.]

It's –

But you know, Mare: it
leaves doubts about *you* –
about who *you are:* nothing
to do with catharsis as far as
vengeance. It has to do with

who you are.

And who *are* you, or who should you be?

Yeah, exactly. Who are you…. Who are you, Jim? Are you the kind of man that can *stand* against this kind of wrong and say it for what it is, and oppose it? Or are you the man who hides behind your mother's skirt all your life.

And you think you've hidden behind your mother's skirt your whole life?

Pretty much… pretty much! I avoided it. I avoided it, I ran away from it, I avoided it…. But I think probably 99.9% of people would do that, too.

Yeah, and I can't say I'd like the 0.1% of the population who'd do different…. I can't say I'd have any respect for someone who'd commit violence against another human being, no matter what the cause.

Oh, okay. [He guffaws.]

In fact, I can say that quite

readily.

Now you see, you depend on *society* to correct the wrongs. You know, sometimes society isn't gonna do it – or isn't doing it.

Well... [sigh]. Well – so you're basically saying that your identity is one of a coward. I mean, that's what you're describing. You're describing yourself as... you're not looking at your achievements, your work, your family. Basically, you're saying your identity is as a coward who failed to live your own life. You are a coward. That's your identity.

Pretty much. Pretty much it is.

ॐ

I will construct an argument based on the notions of bravery provided by Socrates, through Plato, using Laches and Nicias as his interlocutors. I will start with Laches. I will be methodical, logical; I will prove myself, and it, to him. For him, my father, who is not a coward.

My father is 'not-a-coward,' but *not* because he possesses good character – the "endurance with wisdom" to act or resist –

as Laches defined the term. It's true: my father does possess good character. He endured a lifetime without seeking revenge – a lifetime of knowing that his father was murdered solely for political beliefs. My father absorbed that vile knowledge without answering through force; he was acted upon and yet his only reciprocal act was to resist the seduction of violence – that promise of ecstatic catharsis.

It was totally suppressed.

Then what?

In order to resist the appetite of blood, my father created tight-binding rules about exercise and consumption, mistrusting the body's physical impulse. I saw his compulsive resistance and responded with my own logic, namely ten years of anorexia/bulimia. I was a girl who weighed eighty pounds, her muscle eaten from within, feeding on its own organs since meat wasn't given from without; a daughter who swallowed the palpable silence around my family's past; a woman who finally asked: "Tell me about Greece. Tell me what happened there."

The interviews lasted seven years.

ↄ

TAPE #4, SIDE B.
TRANSCRIPT PAGES 46-48.
TORONTO, ONTARIO.
JUNE 1999.
Year One of the interviews, before the narrative's main themes and scenes were clear.

And there was a girl that I knew who died of meningitis. So you were afraid that *you* had it because you were playing with her. Yeah. Because we were playing with her about three or four days before she got sick. And then she got sick and were we exposed. So we were, like, waiting to see what would happen... you know: are you or are you not gonna be all right....

The girl was in your class?

Yeah. And I was very friendly with her, so I went to see her, but they wouldn't let me in except from a hallway. I just peeked in from the hallway.

Do you remember her name?

I remember what she looked like. She was a brunette – long face – a bit of a tomboy, always playing soccer with the boys after school. She was a very good soccer player.... But then she wasn't around. Then word got around that she was very sick. And then you heard it: *'meningitis, meningitis, viral meningitis...'*. That meant she was dead. People who got that died.

So you went to her house. What did you say?

I remember the house. I walked up the stairs – it was a very narrow hallway. And then to my right was a door and there was a bed, and there were all kinds of adults around her, and she was in bed.

Did you go with your mom?

No – I went on my own. In fact, mom told me *not* to go. So I kind of... I went on my own. I walked – it was a good walk.

Did she say anything to you?

No, but she recognized me. She was conscious – she recognized me. I know that.

ॐ

My father is 'not-a-coward,' but *not* because he acted with proper knowledge – "knowledge of what is fearful and what is encouraging" – as Nicias defined the term. Again, it is true that my father acted in this way. As I've argued above, my father knew that violence could provide momentary pleasure; he knew, yet he acted by resisting this temptation.

Nonetheless, action by inaction is inadequate to illustrate my father's status as brave. I need, in addition, a scene in which my father acted despite his expectation of "future evil" and potential harm. This action would be imperative within an ethical framework that places certain values above self-preservation.

It leaves doubts – it does *surprise – you just run.*

My father went to see the brown-haired girl, the tomboy who played soccer with the boys after school. He responded to her, despite his fear of exposure.

❧

TAPE #4, SIDE B.
Continued.

Did you say anything to her?

No, no. Her parents told me
not to come in so I walked
in the side door and walked
up the stairs. It was a narrow
staircase, and then there
was the bedroom – the
sickroom. There were four
or five women hovering
around the bed, where she

was lying. They were old women, you know, with black scarves…. I wanted them to move away so I could see the bed.
And then she saw me – she was conscious – but we didn't exchange any words.

Why did you go? If you know she was contagious…

You go to see whether it was true. You go to make sure that what you hear is true.

To verify the rumours.

To verify and to communicate. You know, you realize what communication meant. *'I'm sorry you're sick, I miss you'*… I didn't get to say that. There were no words. We didn't exchange any words….

You didn't –

But there was recognition, though. There was recognition in her eyes. These were not the 'absent eyes' of meningitis… the delusional, vacant eyes. We saw –

So what –

we saw each other.

So what happened?

So I waited on the stairwell
for a few minutes and the
minute they saw me, they
sent me away. So I went
home.

And what are you thinking on
the way home from an experience like that?

Petrified you're gonna get it.

ɕᴐ

My father, in summary, is 'not-a-coward,' but *not* for the obvious reasons, as stated by Laches and Nicias.

It's true, my father had good character (as evidenced by
his endurance against temptation and indulgence, including
the temptation of vengeance); and he possessed knowledge
which dictated his actions, regardless of potential harm (as
evidenced by his behaviour toward the girl with meningitis).

So why, then, am I still struggling with this question? Why –
despite the fact that he's clearly met the proffered definitions?

Why? Because, as you recall, Socrates never *accepted* those
definitions of bravery. He never *refuted* them – he ravaged the
logic, not the conclusions – nonetheless, he never accepted
them.

What, then, *did* Socrates accept?

What definition of bravery does Socrates allow?

In trying to answer this question, I can't extract lines from the text: I won't find the definition locked inside the words themselves. Instead, I must sense the substance of bravery as it becomes constituted by the dialogue as a whole – by the very process of questioning.

You'd make it a mission in your life.

Is that a worthy mission?

Only by reading and rereading those brief dialogues do I arrive at the definition of bravery: bravery, I realize, is the unceasing examination of the self. Bravery is the endurance, with wisdom, to question one's actions and their underlying arguments. Bravery is asking and acting – proceeding from ongoing, ever-more-precise answers – constructing an internal logic from this knowledge and perception. Bravery is this entrance: the entering into that physical motion of question and exchange.

By this definition, my father is a coward.

But what –

Do I have the guts *to explore it.*

Yeah, exactly.

Who are you?

My father is a coward because he never questioned himself. He never engaged in that steadfast examination of his decisions and motivations, his past and future actions.

My father is a coward.

You are a coward.

Does it surprise you?

I buck at this conclusion; this logic rides me, and I won't accept it. With a violence that Socrates would've chastised – a physical violence which is part of my own logic – I buck at this conclusion and now I know why.

For seven years, my father allowed me to question him. Despite the risks to himself – the risks to his constructed identity, reigned by rules which disallowed desire and memory of past wrongs – my father submitted himself to my questions.

We saw each other: I know that.

My father didn't assume the role of examiner within his life. Instead, he gave that role to me – his daughter – the continuation of his history, the place where past and future could come together, creating understanding within the extension of time. He shaped this role for me, not merely when the interviews began, but much earlier. Through his actions and attitudes, guided by his intuitive ethical framework, my father created my possibility – the possibility for me to have this desire – the desire to examine language and its vital logic.

My father is not a coward.

We have spoken together; we have given the void its unasked questions; we have held this exchange. We are, in this, because he was willing to let his stories come – twisted and surprising – from his body; we are because he trusted me with his words, and I have taken them in my mouth.

Coyote Pup

"Take off your coat."

"There's no room – it's too small!"

"I know. Let's just take off our coats and get into the apartment."

"I don't like it here."

"I know."

"It's too small."

"You said."

He sees his movement in the mirror and stops, captivated. He stares at his reflection wriggling out of its coat.

"Thank you. Now let's take off "

"I'm a Coyote Pup!"

He hops, his hands curled cutely under his chin. In this pose, he's more puppy than coyote; more bunny, really, than pup.

"Are you? You're a 'Coyote Pup'? That's good."

I pluck his outdoor clothes off the floor. One blue mitten is missing. Another goddamn mitten missing.

"Did you have both your mittens when you left the house this morning? Did your daddy give you both mittens?…

Baby?… Are you listening?"

"I'm a Coyote Pup and I'm sad."

He pouts in the mirror, watching himself feel sad.

"Why are you sad, baby?"

"I'm not a baby."

"No, you're right. You're a big boy."

"No I'm not! I'm a Coyote Pup!"

He hops.

"Right. I forgot. You're a Coyote Pup…."

I sigh.

I bend to untie my boots, trying not to bump into my son. The muscles are tight at the back of my knees. I stretch through the tightness, arching the small of my back. This stretch feels good – this lengthening along my tired legs. I've forgotten what 'good' feels like.

It feels like a distant land.

"Why are you sad?" I ask.

"I'm sad."

"Yes…"

My laces lash across my hand. They're sodden with salted water, wicked from the city's sidewalks. The sting seems to flay my skin, which is already chapped.

"But *why* are you sad," I insist.

"Hmm?"

My son hops, hands tucked. He stares. His fingers wiggle and whip in a distinctly non-coyote fashion. They seem like live wires cut from their circuit.

He won't see his father for seven days.

"Hmm?"

"Can you tell me *why* you're sad?"

I sigh again and reach for his hand. He pulls it back; he stares into the mirror.

"I'm sad," he tells himself. "I'm sad because the Mama and Daddy Coyotes got split up. And the Mama Coyote? She moved to a teeny tiny apartment. And the Daddy Coyote? He stayed in the *biiig* big house. And the Boy Pup?" he says. "The Boy Pup, which is me? He didn't like that. He liked it when everybody lived in the big house all together. So the Boy Pup – which is me? – he got sad."

He punctuates this statement with a pout in the mirror.

"Oh, baby..."

I kneel on the unswept floor. I wrap my hands around my son's torso, turning him toward me.

"Baby..."

"I'm not a baby!"

He hops. He mock-licks my face, mimicking the sound of a tongue's swipe across the skin.

"Coyote Pup..."

"Yes!"

He hops. His fingers wiggle.

"Coyote Pup, listen to me: I couldn't stay in the big house. You know that, right?"

He listens intently.

"Why?" he asks.

His intention transforms him. He's trying to understand – to comprehend through story and idea, our human connection.

"Why? Because, when your daddy and I were together, we hurt each other. We fought. Not little fights – not like we have, like you and me, like the last time you were here... Remember? When you wouldn't put on your hat?"

"That was a big fight," he says, quite matter-of-factly.

"Well – but – okay… but it was different," I say.

He pouts.

"That was about a small thing – about putting on your hat. It was *only* about that. *Only* about – although…" I sigh. "It was about power, too, I guess…"

I've lost him. He looks vaguely toward the wall.

"Baby…? Coyote Pup…?" I try again. "Pup, do you remember the fights – the growling? Do you remember the snarling between me and your dad? Baby?…"

I try to snarl, forcing breath over the pith of my palate – a sound that's not shaped by my tongue. I sense him listening. I've made a connection by reflecting his words back to him – his words and tone, just like all the books say. All those countless books on children and divorce, all of which say to listen, to reflect, to reassure.

Step One: Listen to your children. This is harder than you think!

I snarl again.

"Do you remember, Pup?" I say. "It's like the Mama and Daddy Coyotes were trapped in that big house – trapped there together – so they *growled* at each other. They *snarled* and then, I mean, they were starting to *attack* each other! With their claws and teeth and big, strong jaws – they *rrr*ipped at each other. Just *rrr*ipped…"

I feel my son's ribcage expand and contract beneath my hands; his arms hang limp by his sides.

"They were *rrr*ipping and *tear*ing at each other," I say. "And the Mama Coyote was soooo unhappy. She was so tired of the sadness. So she left! She wanted to make a new life for herself so she... She just..."

"What, Mama?" he asks. "What did the Mama do?"

My son stares at me, gently. I feel his body – such a tiny body – held in my hands. He wants to understand.

"Mama?"

I'm not sure how to answer that question, as posed by my three-year-old son: What did I do? What aspect of the story can I give him?

"So she slunk away," I say, "with her tail between her legs."

Step Two: Reflect your children's questions back to them. Let them take the lead! Don't make it more complicated than necessary.

I try again.

"But she dug her own home, right? For herself and her Coyote Pups, whom she loves loves *loves!*... And the home – the den she dug? – it was small, but she made it her own. Right? Coyote Pup?"

Step Three: Reassure!

My son eschews my attempts to look into his eyes, but I don't let him: I move into his line of sight. This is important; I am trying to help him. I am trying to use the allegory that he's created – the story of his family as coyotes, clever and feral – to help him understand what's happened in his life. "She made it her own, right Coyote Pup? Because if she'd stayed?... Coyote Pup?"

"Yeah?"

"If I'd stayed," I say, "we would've torn each other to pieces."

His little heart thumps.

He blinks at me.

He blinks again, three times, in quick succession.

"Really?" my son says. "Really, like, there'd be, like, pieces of your *body* on the *ground*? Like a leg on the ground? Like…"

He lifts his hands, his fingers spreading wide and taut.

"Like fingers all over? Ten of them? All over the *floor?*"

"No, baby. Listen "

"Like blood all over the floor? And jaws all big and strong "

"No, baby… sweetie!"

Listen! Reflect! Reassure! Then shove it up my feral ass: those books are useless.

"Listen, sweetie – please – please listen to me."

I stroke his hair. His curls are damp from sweat; the heater is on too high.

"It's just an expression. A figure of speech. It's like…"

He's gone, without explanation.

He's galloping into the apartment, straight for the small dollhouse which lies on its side, peopled by plastic figurines. The arrangement of these toys hasn't changed in the past seven days, since the morning I'd interrupted my kids' game, hustling them into their snowsuits.

'An iceberg!'

Their father expected my son at 9 A M, once I'd taken my daughter to school; I needed to be prompt.

'It's coming closer!'

All week – this long, quiet week – I'd left the figures unaltered. In them, I could hear the cacophony, my kids' stories entangled and unresolved.

'Look – the iceberg! It's coming toward us!'

My son grabs a large doll whose visage has been broken. One blue eye is sealed shut in a permanent wink, its innocence demented. Face to the floor, it's now an iceberg which, in this version of nature, can move toward the dollhouse, which is a boat.

'The iceberg! It's coming closer!

'Hurry, hurry!'

Last week, the doll was a mountain range in the African plains.

'Hurry – the iceberg!

'Look! Ahhhhh! *Pssshaaaa*.

'Blub blub blub.'

I fill the sink with hot water. The yellow latex gloves snap as I pull them over my chapped hands. The dish soap shoots from the bottle. I watch the bubbles dome and pop.

'We're sinking!'

I start to wash the small stack of dishes: one bowl, one mug, one spoon and the coffee pot. The 'transition days' are the hardest, although the kids don't like to talk about that. No matter how I try to raise the subject, they physically deflect discussion, literally squiggling out of that serious space, unable to focus or settle. "I love you, even when you're not with me," I often say. "I love you," as if those slight words could carry any significance. "I think about you all the time. Okay, babies? You're not responsible, right? You didn't do *anything* wrong. You know that, right? Sweeties? You know that nobody – *nobody* – did anything wrong."

'No! Ahhh!

'Come here! Come here comehere come here! Take the rope!

'But wait!

'*Yes!* The rope!'

The dollhouse floats on the floorboard-sea, somehow res-

117

urrected from its wreckage. All three characters are crowded on the port-side: the princess smiles at the leopard, who's prowling near the knight, who's forever locked in a defensive posture – legs bent, arms spread, body prepared for the coming attack. He's called 'Blueberry' because of the blue emblem on his breastplate.

'Take the rope!

'Unh! *Yes!*

'You got it!

'Yes!'

I unplug the drain in the sink.

'Run to the castle!'

The water gurgles down.

'The castle!'

The castle wasn't part of the story a minute ago; it will disappear when no longer needed.

'Yes!'

The last bubble pops.

My kids' story, I realize, can't ever resolve. In a child's ongoing game, the author – the child – has no distance from the action. From that position – a position without higher perspective – a story can't progress toward its end; the narrative, then, consists completely of play. This is not disturbing for a child.

'No!

'Run!'

"Mama! I want a snack!"

He scrambles up, into the kitchen.

"An apple?"

He nods his head. His tongue is hanging out, his 'paws' tucked beneath the chin.

"Can I cut it for you?"

He nods again. He licks the air.

I wash the apple in the empty sink. I like this, the non-latexed connection of water on skin. It is rare, now: touch. The affair ended two months ago although, technically, it wasn't an 'affair' anymore. Not since I left my husband, abruptly, the day the call came in, one week before Christmas. Exactly one week. The anonymous informant hadn't considered that particular complication: the effect on the children, that vital mythology forever tainted.

Of course, I hadn't considered my children, either. I hadn't considered much of anything. I was simply inside it, right at the tip, my whole life rushing forward – one huge flood contained in that single vein, that single impulse toward the affair – all of my life, right at the tip.

I was such a child.

My hand jerks back. I drop the knife, which clatters onto the floor. I stare at my finger – the clean slice where the skin is separated. I stare, waiting.

"Mama...?"

There is always that moment – that belief, the denial: it is not too deep. There will be no blood.

"Mama, where's my snack?"

I watch as the red bead expands on my finger. The tension keeps the bead intact 'til it grows too large, unable to hold. Then the blood seems to spill out of itself, onto my skin.

I stare, enthralled by its undeniability.

"It's coming, baby..."

"Mama?" My son points to my finger. "Mama, is that where the Daddy Coyote bit you?"

"No, sweetie. No no no – I was just making an allegory.... Like a story, like "

"Maybe it is!" he says. "Maybe the Mama and Daddy Coyotes *rrr*ipped each other apart! And the Mama Coyote – which is you? – she *rrr*an – "

"But!"

" – and dug a *teeny* tiny apartment for the Boy Pup and the Girl Pup and – "

"Baby, listen.... I don't want you to think... Listen to me, okay? I don't want you to think that your daddy would ever *really* hurt me. Do you understand? I don't want – "

He takes a slice of apple off the plate.

"What? The Daddy Coyote?"

"No sweetie. The daddy – *your* daddy – and me. I don't want you to think we'd ever *really* hurt each other. Not like that, not..."

"Oh Mama. You're so silly."

My son bounds toward the couch, scattering the figurines.

"Mama," he says, pouncing onto the cushion. "Mama, can you read me a story?"

He bites the apple with his front teeth.

Coming of Age

She initiated me, showed me certain secrets, made me speak an oath. She was, by all accounts, an unlikely guide. These mysteries were simple to Becky, that 'special' girl; they weren't engulfed in a glorious shame, a toxic pleasure, as they were for me. As they are, still, especially as I write this story.

"I don't want to go," I said.

"Just for two hours."

"I don't like her!"

"I don't care." My mother was chopping an onion, efficient.

"But mom, she's a…" I paused there, pulling the word to the top of my throat.

"*Don't* say it," my mother said.

"But I – "

"You can ride your bike there," she continued. "By yourself, okay? Is it a deal?" She slid the onions into the pan; their sizzle drowned my response.

"I'm gonna bike to the cathedral," I said.

(I said those words. If she didn't hear them, that wasn't my fault.)

"Deal?" she asked.

"Deal."

Within the hour, I was pedaling past Becky's house, heading toward the cathedral's grounds. The landscape was open, sloping, a pastoral rectitude that showcased the chocolaty-brown building. This place wasn't off-limits, exactly; it's just that 'things went on' here.

Things went on: this was all the warning my mother needed to give me when I was younger; the terrain went unexplored for years.

But now I was here, biking through the gates. The single path soon split into four, then eight – diverging, crossing, snaking over contoured hills whose lawns were trim and perfectly shorn. A woman was jogging. The gardeners were mowing. I veered to the left, past a long-limbed churchman on hands-and-knees; he was clipping the stray blades of grass from the path. I didn't slow for him, that lone churchman on all-fours. Instead, I biked fast toward the cathedral itself.

It rose erect, its Gothic spire the tallest structure in our small suburban town. I sped along a path that billowed out, then drew itself acutely inward, toward the church's base where the bushes were most dense.

"Unh..." a Mexican gardener grunted.

I braked abruptly, my bike squealing to a stop. The gardener had stepped onto the path, hauling a large bag of dirt. He turned toward me and halted, as if stricken. I was about to apologize when he puckered his lips and kissed at me. His face became filled with fake longing as he spoke to me – desirously, incomprehensibly – in Spanish.

He was laughing now, joking with his colleague. They

laughed together. They slit into the bags of soil, reaching inside to toss fistfuls of fertilized dirt under the bushes. The smell was overwhelmingly mineral.

Once I'd arrived at the other side of the church, I dumped my bike flat on the grass and approached the bushes. Kneeling down, I crawled through an opening, ducking beneath the branches. When I stood, my lavender corduroy pants were covered in fresh earth. I brushed them off and stood stupidly, not knowing what to do now that I was here.

I looked around. The place was pungent and hidden; it was cramped tight, the bushes tangled, unruly beside the shaft of the church. I looked up. My head dropped back, stretching the front of my neck 'til it strained. I tried to swallow but couldn't: my voice box wouldn't slide through that stretched space, my throat arched back. I tried again, wanting that uncomfortable pause – that physical pressure in my throat – and that's when I saw them: two shapes protruding from the side of the building. They were brown, with beak-like noses, haunches firm and tongues grotesquely out. I stared at the gargoyles. My voicebox was stopped at the top of my soft palate and I breathed. I watched as more figures appeared. Dozens now, perched all over, one body leading to another – bellies, haunches, spiked tails and open mouths – everywhere bulging, pressing for me to see.

The gardeners drove away. I heard the men laugh, freely.
It was then that I swallowed.

ও

Her mother was making cookies that day. She stood at the

island in the emerald-coloured kitchen, her palms pressed on the counter. The ingredients were arrayed beside the cookbook, whose pages were warped from an earlier spill.

"How much is a pint?" she asked, annoyed.

"A pint is a pint," Becky answered. I watched as she ate peanut butter from the jar, sucking her finger then sticking it back in. A pale green slug of snot was suspended on her upper lip. She snorted; it disappeared.

"A pint is a pint – right? – a pint!" She delighted in her singsong chant. "A pint is a pint – right? – a pint! A pint is a pint is a right is a pint!"

Becky's eyes were blue, her hair blonde. Blonde hair and blue eyes: that was the prettiest, I'd always said, as if those colours conferred the essence of Barbie. I was at an age, almost, when I'd stopped playing with dolls and stuffed animals.

"A pint is a pint is a pint, alright? A pint is a pint is a pine is a tree is a pea is a nut is a – want some?"

Becky thrust her finger deep into the goopy-thick peanut butter, stirring with a tight motion of her hand. "Huh? Want some? Huh? You're not answering me!" Becky stamped her foot. "Mommy! She's not answering me!"

Her mother cursed at the cookbook. "What the fuck…"

"Mommy mommy mommy ma…" Becky seemed enamoured of this new sound. She played with it, toyed with it, her lips remaining flaccid at the end: "Mommy mommy mommy ma… Mommy mommy mommy ma…"

"One second, okay, Becky? One second."

Becky was three years older than me. We went to the same school, although she was housed in the 'Special Ed' program with all the other kids like her: the other 'Special' kids; the other kids who fit in that gap, that pause, the potent hesitation.

My mother forbade me to say the word. I must say 'Special,' she warned, even though I'd *mean* that other word. Even though both words would *mean* the same thing – the same people – the same strange way they laughed when nothing was funny, and stared while everyone else was learning not to look (not directly); the way, too, they made noises and bleeps and huffs as if we couldn't hear – as if they could just say and do whatever came into their minds, which were dumb.

Those kids rode to school, all together, in a small special bus.

"No thanks, Becky," I answered. "I don't want – "

"Mommy!"

" – any."

"She said no! She said NO!"

Becky's mother banged her fist on the counter. "What is it!" Her pink headband held back her hair; I could see the line where her face changed colour – where the makeup ended and her skin began. "What's the problem!" She shoved the cookbook, starting a chain reaction.

"Mommy-mommy!" Becky said, pointing to the counter's edge; her finger was slick with peanut butter smoothed by saliva. "Mommy-mommy!"

"Shit!"

The cookbook, which was shoved by Becky's mom, had pushed the bowl, which had pushed the bag of flour, which now was falling.

"Fuck!"

Her mother continued to curse, a whole long list of forbidden words.

"God *damn* it!"

Becky clapped as the bag of flour burst. She said it was pretty, like snow before the dogs had pissed on it.

∽

The visits continued, once a week for two months, each one with this same pattern: argue with my mom, bike to the cathedral, get through the hours with Becky. Spring grew warm during those weeks. The Mexican gardeners swooned when they saw me; they also swooned at mothers who jogged past, their bodies zipped tight in pink track suits. The gargoyles vomited water on the days after rain.

During that time, I celebrated my twelfth birthday, excluding Becky from the party, of course. My friends gave me pop music cassette tapes (*Strip, Like a Virgin, Love is a Battlefield*, etc.) all wrapped with pink paper and scissor-curled plastic ribbon. In the same week as my birthday, the cathedral's bushes budded then bloomed: lilac, pink, fuchsia, yellow. For the first time, I was drawn to the yellow bushes most. The pink flowers, always my favourite, now seemed stupidly obvious. Unlike the pink's insipid hue, the yellow petals seemed alluring, saturated – so fully saturated, their colour threatened to drip into liquid. I crushed a petal between my fingers; the pigment stained my skin.

By the end of the month, the bushes had turned shaggy with green leaves. That's when the kids from high school found fertilized pockets of privacy and I found them doing 'things' under the drooping branches. One of my friends, whose sister was in high school, whispered about 'oral sex'; I imagined those kids there, at the cathedral, kissing with their faces suctioned: *oral sex*. I imagined them kissing, then talking, and talking, and talking, and I didn't know what she meant by 'zipper fuck' but I didn't ask. I didn't even make that sound with my mouth: *zipper fuck*.

༺

The last time I went to Becky's house, she was dancing outside, on a marble pedestal beside the front stairs. Her ringletted blonde hair was frizzed in the humidity.

"Hey Marianne! What's black and white and red all over?" Her pelvis punched up three times: *red – all – o*ver. She moved like a Solid Gold dancer: lewd without any allure.

"I don't know," I said.

"A newspaper!" she squealed. "It's *read* all over!" She hopped and clapped. "It's *read!*" She wiggled (all over), ending with her hands on her hips, one knee bent, chest thrust out. "Hey Marianne!" she called.

"What."

"How many balls can a boy carry?"

"I don't know."

"Three! One in his hands and two in his sacs! Hey Marianne!"

"What."

Becky stopped her compulsive squirm-dance. "Marianne? Where do beavers live?"

"Beavers?" I asked, bored. I straddled my bike seat, sliding imperceptibly to the right, reminding myself of the pleasant sensation I'd recently discovered. "I dunno…" My thin flip-flops dug into the gravel driveway; their thong cut into the skin between my toes.

"I can't remember," she continued. "Because bears live in a cave and wolves live in a den but I can't remember where beavers live…. Bears, wolves, beavers… bears, wolves, beavers… where do beavers live? Marianne! Where do –"

"In a dam."

"A what?"

"A dam."

"No, you're wrong."

"It's a *dam*, Becky."

Her eyes bulged. "Ooooo," she said, lewd and squirming.

"What…?"

"Dam…" She articulated clearly now, her mouth working itself distinctly. "Dam … dam … damn … damn … *you* said a curse!" She bit her bottom lip, her half-smile curved, exaggerated in its glee. "Oooo, you said a curse, you bad girl."

And it was nothing, really. I said a curse: 'damn.' So what.

"So what," I said. I was flushing, filled with her accusation. So what: I said a curse. My first curse: so what.

"So I never *knew* you were a bad girl." She giggled, bringing her fingers to her lips, covering her mouth with one hand. With the other, she clutched at her skirt, hitching it up her thigh. Her panties were lavender, lined in pink.

I shifted on my bike seat as she jumped off the pedestal. She said she had a trick she wanted to show me.

❧

I never told my mother why I wouldn't go back.

"Come on," she said, dismissive. "Two hours a week. How bad could it be."

"I won't go."

"Marianne, how bad –"

"I won't –"

"Why not!"

I spoke the rest slow, so slow: teeth bared, lips swollen and apart. "Because," I said, "she's a fucking retard." I stared, defending those words.

"What - did - you - say?"

"I said," – grotesque – "she's a fucking retard."

I stomped up the stairs, to my bedroom, which looked like hers. There, where she'd lain on her plush carpet, panties off, chuffing. The muscles were tight on her face, a succession of grimaces; nothing was loose except that sound from down, that wet and slurp. I stared at her face so as not to see the dark hair and then the pink. But I couldn't help but sense it. You can't help but sense it: that twitchy motion, the deeper motion, the slow wave that filled me. Her breath was soft and panting.

She offered me her fingers to smell afterward. To taste. Then she put them in her mouth and skipped downstairs.

"Do you want some peanut butter?" she called.

☙

And it's nothing, really: a coming-of-age story, unconscionably vile in its baldness and honesty. It's nothing, except for one vital fact – the fact that this story is mine, and I choose to tell it. I choose to let it fill me with my necessary shame.

Like A Cat

I danced for the money, an envelope packed with cash: that's obvious.

But it was more than that.

I danced for the experience, the sensations I'd know physically, fully, only if I tried it.

That's incorrect.

I danced to seduce him.

Close: I'm closer now.

I danced to seduce him with the story I'd tell – the way I'd use the story to bring him to me, the woman, the character portrayed.

Yes: I was dancing for the story, but I never got the chance to tell him.

KALENDAR BAR, TORONTO, ONTARIO. MARCH 2008.

"So they actually switched places."

"They did not!"

"Oh, but they did…. The woman actually forced her boyfriend to get up and face the wall so he couldn't see me dancing."

I'm describing a scene from the previous night, a busy Friday at Opa Taverna, where I bellydance.

"I knew she was trouble the minute I started my set," I say.

"Ah, but you like trouble."

"Sometimes."

I met him three months ago, though we'd been noticing each other for weeks. I kept seeing him at a local café where we'd both be drinking coffee, reading philosophy: me, Lacan; he, Žižek. We'd peer at each other, a tacit but tentative acknowledgement. "We should switch books," I finally said one day. He was reading *The Plague of Fantasies*; I was reading *On Feminine Sexuality, The Limits of Love and Knowledge*. "We should exchange names," he replied. He extended his hand.

"I always make a 'mysterious' entrance," I continue. "I'm draped in a veil, almost completely covered, and the song starts with a single note that gets louder and louder –"

"Building in tension."

"Exactly," I say. I am overexcited. This is my first date in two years, and I'm not even sure it's really a 'date.' "So I'm walking on stage, but I'm not supposed to stay on stage," I tell him. "I'm supposed to dance among the tables, providing an 'exciting dining experience.'" I quote the phrase with my fingers.

"Who tells you this?"

"Tony, the manager.... He's a piece of work," I say.

I tell him about the wall of 'celebrity photos,' circa 1983: Tony with Susan Sarandon, Brooke Shields, Madonna, Cher. All of these women tower over Tony; they seem like goddesses beside him, strength emanating from their very teeth. "Tony always looks somewhat afraid...."

"I don't blame him!"

We laugh at the ridiculousness of that place.

The waitress refills our wine glasses. She inquires whether we need anything.

"No," he says. "Everything is perfect."

I smile. I'm a little nervous about the cost of the wine, but I'll worry about that later. This is not the time to think about such things.

"So the first day I worked there –"

"How long have you been working there?"

"Two years," I say. Ever since I left my husband. "So my first night," I continue, "Tony tells me, 'They can put tips in your waistband but not in your bra. If they give the tip to the bartender, for you, she gets to keep half.'"

"Half?"

"I know! It's absurd! But get this: Tony says, 'If the bartender gets a tip for you,' – and this bartender is gorgeous, mind you… young and voluptuous – 'if she gets the tip, she *might* give you a shot of ouzo, if you ask her right.'"

"And do you ask her right?"

"Always," I say.

He sits back. This flurry demands a brief pause. He sips his wine and I watch him. "This is excellent wine," he says.

I don't tell him, of course, that I use Opa's tips to pay my rent. These tips are worth more on alternate weeks – the weeks when my kids are with their dad, and I don't need to pay for a babysitter. These facts, however, are not worth mentioning. They would alter the tone of the story; they would ruin the mood.

"Anyway, I'm marking my territory, and –"

"You're *what?*"

"I'm marking my territory."

"Marianne, you must explain."

"This story is going to take forever!"

He looks at his watch. "We've got time," he says.

My finger circles the rim of the wine glass. "Do we?" I ask.

"A little," he says. It is quiet for a moment. "Keep going, Marianne... please..."

He pours more wine; he raises his glass.

"I'm waiting," he says.

"Timing is everything," I reply.

I tell him, then, about 'marking my territory.' The phrase comes from a bellydance workshop I'd attended, run by a famous dancer from L.A. "Picture it," I say. "Twenty women are sitting on the floor, fawning at the feet of this dancer."

We were taking a break. She was telling us stories.

She performed for the Jordanian Queen, I tell him; apparently, the Queen is a 'tigress in bed.'

"That's good to know," he says.

"Oh, Laila was filled with all sorts of insider info."

"Like...?"

"Well, bellydancers in Lebanon wear spiked heels and sequins, and most of them have breast implants," I say. "And dancers in Japan can earn more if they start in a kimono and strip during the course of their show."

"I never knew...."

"But you could've guessed."

"I could guess at all sorts of things."

"And of course," I say, ignoring this comment. "Of course, she talked about love." Her lost love, an Egyptian intellectual who wanted her to stop performing.

"'He could not imagine me dancing for another man....'" I say. I perform the words, using a fake Arabic accent – no more fake than Laila's was. "'If another man *looked* at me while I was dancing,' she said, 'he would *kill* himself with the *passion* of his jealous rage! He would *tear* that man with his bare hands! Just *thinking* about it made him want to *ravish* me!'"

'Did he, Laila?' a girl asked.

"She actually had tears in her eyes when she asked that!"

"Oh, you bellydancers are filled with emotion."

"We're brimming with it," I say, with pitch-perfect irony. "And what's even better?" I say. "The dancer whose eyes welled up? She's a girl name Vicky from Peterborough, Ontario, who goes by the stage name of 'Voula.'"

"That's too much," he says.

I don't tell him that Vicky is a beautiful dancer; I've already made her a joke.

"So then we got back to work," I say.

It was an advanced workshop, for women who were already performing. Laila was helping us to shape our set, to think about the performance as a whole.

"So Laila says, 'At the beginning of your set, you must mark your territory...' And she's walking in a circle, really close to us." I'm circling my hand. My wrist is supple; I'm somewhat drunk. "And we're mesmerized."

"And all she's doing is walking?"

"Oh, but the *way* that she's walking." One arm up, fingers holding a corner of the veil; the other arm forward, softly curved before her. "We can only see her eyes. The rest of her body is hidden by the veil. And she's prowling."

"She's stalking you."

"Yes… She's taking every step very slowly…"

"Slow – "

" – and inevitable."

"Yes."

And all of us, almost imperceptibly, took a step back. And again. "It's as if she were commanding us," I say.

"She was commanding you, Marianne."

He smiles at me. He sips his wine. The ring on his finger glows warm beside the goblet.

"'You must mark your territory,'" I say, leaning forward, "'like a cat.'"

OPA TAVERNA, TORONTO, ONTARIO. APRIL 2008.

I'm chit-chatting with the bouzouki player at a small table near the bar. I find him here, drinking espresso sadly, whenever I arrive at Opa.

"How's it going, Spiros?"

"The crowd is dead."

Spiros is a short man, balding, with very hairy arms. He is an excellent bouzouki player. From an instrument known for its cocky flash, Spiros can coax longing and desire.

Tony wants flash. He said this to Spiros last week.

"Fast fingers make money," Tony said.

"Fast fingers do not make love," Spiros replied. He meant it sincerely.

Spiros stirs his espresso with his little spoon. He talks about his young son, whom he sees on Saturdays, Wednesdays, and every other Sunday. Spiros' ex-wife is getting remarried next week.

"Marianna," Tony says. He shakes my hand and gives me

the keys to the 'change room' downstairs. This is actually the employee closet, with a toilet stuck in the corner."How's the crowd tonight?" I ask. "I hear they're not-so-lively out there."

"They're fine," Tony says. "They just need a little wine, a little meat." Tony squints his eyes. "Which costume did you bring?"

"The burgundy one."

"Oreaia." Tony winks.

Tony likes the burgundy costume: the slit is long on the skirt, and the bra is braided in golden rope. "A little meat, a little wine: that's all they need."

I head toward the stairs, past the wall of celebrity photos.

"Marianna," Tony calls, "Table 6 just ordered three more bottles of wine, okay?" Tony's trinity of fingers brush together; I'm not sure I've read the gesture right – assuming there's a gesture to read at all. But then he winks and so I know.

"Thanks for the tip," I say.

Tony nods absentmindedly: he's already conferring with the Sri Lankan busboy while snapping, simultaneously, to grab the attention of the uni-browed waiter from Sparta.

In all this time, I have not noticed the man at the bar, though he forms the crux of this story.

"Are you ready?" the bartender asks a few minutes later. She cues the CD as I stand, in costume, at the top of the stairs.

"One second," I say.

A waiter is walking by with a tray of cheese that he'll soon set on fire. This is the house specialty: *Opa!* "Can you wait 'til I'm done with my intro?" I ask. "Before you light the cheese...?"

"Are you ready or what?" The bartender chews her gum

with an open mouth.

"Because of the veil?" I persist.

The waiter looks at me with his handsome Macedonian face.

"Because I spin with the veil, so…."

"No," he says.

The music begins.

"It's on!" the bartender calls. She blows a bubble.

I am not up for this gig tonight.

The note crescendos, expanding through the room. Spiros nods at me. "*Ela*, Marianna," he says. I drink his encouragement like nectar. "*Oreaia*."

"*Efharisto*, Spiros," I say.

My eyes glide over the audience as I enter. I see them watch me. I prowl and our gazes connect; I let go. I dismiss them; I hold them. I mark my territory.

I think of how I'd describe this to him – this professor of literature who often talks of the 'male gaze;' who often allows his gaze to stray.

What would I tell him, I think as I walk.

I'd put it in terms that would excite his mind: who's seeing whom; who's predator, who's prey. I'd talk about the veiled dancer and all the diners, staring and waiting, wanting her while she stalks them. She prowls, but she knows she must do as she's told. She's in a position of servitude.

I'd tell him this.

I look at the people who watch me enter, my body draped in a golden veil.

He'd sip his wine.

He'd mention a philosopher, quoting Nietzsche, perhaps,

on the cruel desire that must exist between worthy adversaries; he'd make it erotic but pretend that it wasn't. "Can you separate cruelty from eroticism?" he'd ask. Or maybe he'd mention Heidegger: the mutual presence of subject and object, gazing at each other like two perfect mirrors. Reflections of the self in the other who sees, in you, his essence reflected; a fast scintillation that shimmers, faster, quickening until it ruptures.

Professors of literature like the word 'rupture,' I think to myself.

And all the while – all while I think about flirting, with him, in terms of philosophy – I'm prowling barefoot on a stage at a restaurant where cheese is in flames and a fork is lying, prongs up, in the middle of the floor.

"Focus, sweetheart," I whisper to myself. I hear the words echo inside the veil.

I focus.

"Opa," a woman says. She is busty with large dark eyes and overly-stylized hair. She swirls her glass and smells the wine, inhaling deep. Table 6.

I start to spin.

The single note is expanding as I rise onto tiptoe. The veil lifts and I arch back, raising my chest toward the ceiling. I spin, giving a glimpse to all in the room.

"Opa," the woman repeats.

And the note explodes, shattered by the driving rhythm of the song.

'Chicky-chicky, boom-boom,' the young men chant. Oh yes: this song gets everyone going. I stop my spin, exact on the *boom*, and stand with my chest toward Table 6. One leg is forward, thrust through the slit in my skirt. I shimmy-walk toward the women, leaving the veil in a pool on the stage. The Spartan waiter knows he must retrieve it.

Song #2 takes me to Table 8, where a Greek family dines: four generations, all together. I start with the adolescent girl whose body is beginning to ripen. I give her a gentle shoulder roll, but she evades my gaze, ashamed by the sensuality of the dance. I pause, posing as the music flips into its refrain; I hold my pause, almost too long, then I mermaid toward a woman whose toddler sits on her lap. She bounces the baby, clapping the girl's hands together. Her husband tickles his daughter's chin, then kisses his wife on the cheek. As he does, I punctuate the mermaid with a hip-beat, sharp; then he whispers in his wife's ear, biting her on the earlobe.

I watch his teeth on her skin.

I shimmy hard, with a playful pelvic thrust, up on the beat.

"Opa," I whisper, and the woman puts her hand on her husband's thigh.

I'm about to move away, to mingle with another table, when I notice an elegant, older woman who's fishing through her purse. She takes out a twenty and calls me over. With red-painted nails, she slips the money into my waistband. She gestures toward her father, who sits at the head of the table.

Of course: the *papou*. I love the *papous*. These guys are glorious: frisky, but completely unthreatening. They appreciate what I do; they like the grinds, the scoops, the deep undulations. It reminds them.

"I'm ninety years old today!" the *papou* says. He taps his cane, precise on the beat.

"You look gorgeous," I tell him and shimmy my shoulders. I pause as he places some money in my bra. I hope that Tony hasn't noticed. "Happy birthday," I say, and blow him a kiss.

By Song #4, I'm working the other side of the room. To-night, it's dominated by a table of young middle-American tourists. I down-hip shimmy-walk toward a group of three boys, then I settle into a loose, fat shimmy – a motion that slowly constricts, still wet but gripping as the music heightens. My hands start to rise along my torso, separated from my skin by the merest distance: up, along my chest to my neck and face, and now my hair. I touch it. I muss my hair, shaking my head back-and-forth, my fingers soft and swirling. I close my eyes. My shimmy comes tighter, faster, till I slip into vibration; my legs now move in unison, convulsing the body.

"This octopus is really good!" a girl says. "Isn't it, honey?"

With that, I release as if heaved from my trance. I let my hands fall. One lies limp at my side while the other rests on my forehead. I pant, feigning disorientation from this intense, internal erotic journey.

I pant, because this move is extremely difficult.

A girl giggles. Her finely curved lips are frosted pink. "She got all *crazy* just now!" she says with her lovely, useless lips. "Did you see that?" She grabs her fiancé's hand; the diamond on her finger is ugly and uncommonly large.

"I did, sweet pea!" he says as he chomps the last piece of deep fried squid. He licks his fingers.

"But she doesn't have big knockers!" another boy says. "Bellydancers are supposed to have big knockers!"

"Hush up!" a girl twitters. She slaps him lightly on the arm.

I will tell him about this, I think to myself.

I will make them characters, caricatures: fifteen blonde girls and beefy boys whose collective fantasy of exotic adventure takes them to Toronto, to the wilds of ethnic Greektown. I will portray them cruelly, with all the irony inherent in using them like that – using people for my story.

Tony peers at me from the bar. He nods to Table 6; I shimmy away from the American tourists.

"Bye-bye!" one says.

I turn, quick, to lock my gaze on hers. I give one slow chest circle; she blushes crimson, her smile fading. Satisfied, I continue to Table 6.

My final song has begun: a fast Greek *rembetiko*. I approach the table, right up close, then I undulate away. As I do, I point to the busty woman with the pearl necklace; I beckon her toward me, pulling her forward with each undulation. She responds. Without hesitation, the whole table is standing, shaking their way toward the stage.

These women are fantastic. I dance among them, snaking through their revelry. The buxom woman grabs my veil and flings it around a man from a neighbouring table. He gulps his wine and they dance together. The whole place is cheering, clapping – including the teenaged girl.

"Opa!" the *papou* calls with a raucous voice. By the end of the song, he is standing in the centre of the stage; all the women are dancing around him. He lifts up his cane in a gesture of victory or joy. This is how my performance ends.

"*Oreaia!*" Spiros says as I walk downstairs. He smiles at me; even his smile is sad.

While I wait for Tony to pay me, the bartender gives me a free shot of ouzo and fifty bucks, cash. "From the ladies at Table 6," she says. I smile and thank her with all the sarcasm I can conjure.

I sip the ouzo.

The man is seated beside me – the man on whom this story hinges.

"Your movement is very controlled," he says.

I can't quite place his accent, the breathy softness of his tongue.

"I've seen many dancers," he continues. "They all have their specific skill. Yours is control."

"You think so?" I say. "That's my specific skill?" I'm not in the mood for flirtation. But this man is very attractive: dark eyes, thick hair, smooth caramel skin. He is also wearing a Rolex watch, which does not appear to be fake.

I swivel my chest toward him, just slightly, my right shoulder pulled back.

"Most definitely," he says. "It is your control."

I drink my ouzo while we talk. Spiros is singing mournfully – a song about a woman abandoned on a rock by her lover. Tony is yelling at the sous-chef; I can see him in the kitchen, gesticulating through the steam from a massive pot of pasta.

"I am a bellydance aficionado," the man says. "I travel all over the world for my work. I like to sample the dance wherever I go."

"I hear it's wild in Lebanon," I say.

"It's a freak show in Lebanon."

"You don't like high heels?"

"I like a woman's natural body... her natural beauty... I like your control," he repeats. Then he makes his proposition.

"Think about it," he says. "Call me tomorrow."

He gives me his card; he is, apparently, an executive at a large international bank.

"Okay," I reply. "I'll think about it."

He slips his fine leather wallet into his pants. "I'll see you tomorrow," he says. Then he's gone, out the door, leaving me without a tip.

It would make a good story, I say to myself. I sit at the bar, waiting for Tony to pay me.

QUEEN WEST GALLERIES, TORONTO, ONTARIO.
MAY 2008.

He holds the door open for me. I walk inside the long gallery. When I don't hear his footsteps, I glance over my shoulder. I gaze at him while I walk away. I see him watching; I watch him as he lets himself get caught.

We look at the gothic photos in the gallery: beautiful woman with angel wings, arranged in sado-masochistic poses. Nothing special, we agree.

We soon move on, walking east on Queen Street. It is the first warm day of spring. My skin is bathed in golden sunlight; it feels like a promise. "I have the strangest story to tell you," I say. But my timing is off; we're now entering another gallery. This one is filled with artful photos of a nudist colony. The story will wait.

We browse through the gallery separately, each of us contemplating the artwork: photographs of men and women, blithe or posing; children playing; old people waltzing, all of them nude. I glide through the gallery, aware of him circling, stopping to consider a photo – leaning close or stepping back, his hands clasped behind him. In time, we come together before a vertical photo of a teenaged girl.

She stands in the shower. The water pours down as she

smoothes back her hair, her elbows spread. She stares at the camera defiantly.

"She is very physically present," I say.

I feel him beside me, looking at the girl.

"She is," he says.

I have never seen this man with a partner. I often see him walking in our neighbourhood, biking, but always alone. His wife, whom he's never mentioned in the months we've been innocently meeting, seems an abstraction to me; she is merely an idea which never takes shape in my mind. This is not an excuse, only a fact.

I lean toward him.

"She's lovely."

We are not touching but I sense the distance between us. This is, in itself, a form of contact: this wall of delicious resistance.

I want to break it.

I walk away from the photo.

"You said you had a crazy story," he says as we step outside, heading toward the park.

"Right – I almost forgot," I say.

I start to set it up. "So I see him sitting at the bar, but I don't really pay attention. I'm doing my entrance, marking my –"

"You told me about that," he says. He's looking at a woman who strolls past, wearing a tank top and low-slung shorts.

He does not mention Nietzsche or Heidegger.

"Right… sorry…" I say. "So he's at the bar, and the women at Table 6 are drinking…. One of them is very intent on the dance," I say. "It's her birthday."

It's the birthday of the gorgeous woman at Table 6. The

woman with her hair cut blunt, in a seriously sexy bob, wearing a simple necklace – a silver chain with a large pearl that hung low on her chest, pendulous. This is what I tell him.

I touch my chest where the pearl would be.

I've got his attention now.

"So I'm finishing my set, and this guy's at the bar."

"I thought of you the other day," he says.

"What?"

He sits on the ground beneath a tree. He slips off his sandals.

"You thought of me?" I say.

I sit beside him; we both lie down, stretched on the grass.

"You think of me?"

"I was reading Nietzsche."

I smile. Let go, I think to myself; it will all play out as it must. *Amor fati.*

He is talking about *Zarathustra*, about Nietzsche's worship of the female dancer. Everyone associates Nietzsche with music, he says – the Dionysian pull into base desire, the pulse from which life's primal force arises inside us. A shameful place, when viewed in the light of logic and reason. But the dancer, he says: the dancer, for Nietzsche, embodies both beauty *and* eroticism. She is not an Apollinian figure, radiant and otherworldly. No, she is distinctly human: fertile, fecund, profusely powerful.

"I found myself thinking of you," he says.

His toes are now touching my leg. This is the first true contact we've ever had; it is excruciatingly light.

My hand floats on the blades of grass. I can't bring myself to look at him. I listen to his voice; I listen to the breeze, this beautiful warmth.

"It's a beautiful dance," I say. "I should perform for you some time.... We could easily arrange that."

He pauses. His foot stops moving.

"Would you like that?" I ask.

"Meredith used to take bellydance," he says.

His foot remains on my leg. I feel it there, completely inert.

I don't tell him about the private dance.

I don't tell him how it was to arrive at the man's hotel suite. To be ordered, immediately, to apply more makeup. To be told I needed to dance on a chair.

I don't tell him how it was to see the stack of bills, more money than I'd earned for my forthcoming novel. He counted the money before I began; when I reached to take it, he held it aloft. He wagged his finger, shaking his head. "After," he said.

I do not tell him this version of the story.

Nor do I tell him what I had intended: I don't become an insouciant character – a woman who's far more seductive than I'll ever be. I, Marianne, can't ever embody the eroticism of that woman except, of course, when I tell him the story; then, in the telling, I am pure pleasure.

But I don't get to do this: I don't get to tell him. And it's all because he stated her name and, in so doing, she became real.

You

Four stories I had: four memories of my father. You made me say them there, beside the waterfall, close to the pit where the apples decay. We'd been there earlier in the week: you and me. You, beautiful: wildly beautiful. Like the roses I cut as we walked up the mountain: too painfully beautiful. I cut them for you. I gave them with disgust.

I gave you my stories, too. Four stories: a finite number, a small number. They were mine until you asked for my voice, there by the waterfall. You and me and your father, all together. You between us, seeking the story: the great tragedy of the Greek Civil War. Yes? This is what you wanted? The tragic Greek story, brought to its climax by you. Yes?

Vulgar: you were vulgar to violate that sacred boundary.

And so: Story Number One.

The thing I remember is this: there was a well in the middle of a wheat field. The wheat was quite high, so I couldn't see the well. And we were walking. Me and the men. They were day labourers, working the fields: wheat, tobacco, corn. At one point my father lifted me up and said, 'There is it. There, Yianni, you can see the well.' And I remember that: I remember the rise above the wheat. Above the men. Dunked in light, my father's hands around my body.

This is one of my stories.

This I told you, all of this: that small story, those finite sentences. I told you there by the pit: the farmer's compost pit, where he gathered the apples to rot. But you wouldn't remember that, would you? The pit where you crouched low, your long skirt filthy, its hem heavy with mud. You wouldn't remember that: you were drunk in the middle of the afternoon. Drunk in this foreign place where nothing made sense, where all was exotic: the music, the food, the language. Everything touched you directly here: the sunlight, the scents. The soil.

I watched you get on hands and knees and breathe the decay with your mouth.

But that was our first visit to the waterfall, before your father arrived. Then, you weren't conducting research; then you were gathering experience. Though maybe they're the same to you? Perhaps?

But back to me: four stories. Four memories of my father. Told beside the waterfall, translated by your father: my memories, through him, for you.

A potent situation. Exciting, yes?

This must've been exciting for you: a writer, an American girl. A tragic scene: the waterfall, the men, two sides of the story. And you, so young, luring us there with your needs. Your 'need to understand,' you said. To 'know this terrible history.'

And let me ask you, Marianna: Do you even know what I gave you? Can you even recall the hands? Firm hands: the hands of a rebel. A true man.

I thought you understood: that first visit, I thought you

knew. But it didn't end there. You brought me back, that second visit, me and you and your father. You asked your questions: your thin, little questions, your father translating. You sat on that dirt and you asked.

And you know, Marianna, I never did see the well. In Story Number One, the well itself was unimportant, except that it led to the rise: the rise, the submission, the hands on the body. The hands of a rebel. I thought you understood.

Story Number Two.

I didn't see my father in this second story. He was with the rebels by then. The guerrillas. He was a Communist. And I know: I said, that day, that my father couldn't possibly have killed other men. I said this to your father, but that was a lie.

There's no need to hurt him, right Marianna? Why would we want to hurt your father.

But the truth is, I'm sure my father killed Conservatives. He was a Communist and it was a war. A brutal war, the Civil War. You understand that, don't you, Marianna? They used their guns on men. On women, too: the shaft on the thigh, lifting the skirt. They were rebels and it was war.

So I didn't see him in this second story because he was a rebel. But I knew he was nearby. That's what makes this a story: my father's proximity to me.

And don't roll your eyes: *don't*. Though you did that day, by the waterfall. You rolled your eyes because it was too much for you. The bareness of this story: yes, it is sordid, I know. This story's nakedness is sordid, like pain without the sweetness. But *don't*, Marianna, insist on hearing the stories if you lack to ability to listen.

Yes?

You listened so much better that first time. Remember? The first time, without words, you knew how to carry my suffering. You cradled my memories and I was, for a single moment, released. Yes: you gave me that reprieve. That beautiful exhaustion. I thought, that first time, that you understood.

But now: Story Number Two. In its naked entirety, Story Number Two.

I was eating dinner: chicken cooked by my grandmother. I finished my portion and said 'I would like some more.' And my grandmother said, 'No, Yianni. The rest is for your father.'

And that was it. That was how I knew my father was close by.

'*The rest is for your father.*' That one night, we shared hunger for the same food. We both wanted that meat and I denied myself for him: my own father. Because he was close by. And it was true, Marianna: he was there that night. While I was asleep, he came to the house. In the morning, I saw the bones pried apart, cleaned by his teeth.

And that is my story, my second memory of my father.

It's pathetic, no? This is what you think: that I am pathetic. That I like to play the victim.

But I *was* the victim, wouldn't you say, Marianna? My mother dead of pneumonia; my father encamped with the rebels; the government soon collecting me, taking me to the orphanage where I was 're-educated.' This is the life of a victim, no? You sensed that? You sensed and responded to me, as a victim. The injured man. The strong, impenetrable man who has, inside, a softness. An injury. And only *you* can see it. And because you see it, Marianna, you reach to touch it: this palpable injury. Only you can touch the wound and heal it with your hands.

Yes? You thought you could do this? This was your response to me, your uncle: the Communist. Yes?

You were so transparent, Marianna. The young often are. But don't be ashamed: you're not the only one. Maria, my beautiful Maria, she responded too. Decades ago, when we were kids. A wild time: university in the 1960s, when Greece was ruled by the dictators. When we were driven by pure ideals: pure, abstract ideals. 'Justice,' 'democracy,' 'freedom': pure abstraction coupled with the body.

It was a wild time, and I was her project. Her Communist. She gave me her books because I couldn't afford to buy my own. She slipped me cash, which her parents lavished on her even as she marched in Syntagma Square, shouting slogans against 'Capitalist pigs.' Even still, she took their cash. And I'm not sure she was aware of the contradiction.

I, though: I was aware.

In her apartment, I'd prepare opulent meals. She would study and I would cook, her scent still wet on my beard. Yes? And then I'd serve her, my Maria. I'd interrupt her work, make her eat this excessive meal: I'd watch her eat, excessively. I was aware, then: we were eating Capitalist money.

Your family's money.

She was beautiful then, my Maria. She was wild.

Am I a victim?

I, the son of a Communist, raised in an orphanage. I, who was watched by the government: your daddy's Conservative Government that kept a file on me. A thick, official file that they'd consult whenever I applied for anything: a passport, a job, graduate school. All were denied because of my file.

Do you understand what this means?

Maria understood.

Maria loved that I was denied. That I was a victim and a villain: a Communist who would punish her for her privilege. A rebel who'd suck her pure, abstract pretensions till she bled. Yes? This you understood.

But don't mistake me, Marianna: she loved me, too. My wife loves me. It's just that. Beneath this love between two people lies a thick, slathered layer of animosity.

I am the son of a Communist.

She is the daughter of a Conservative.

These are our roles. We play them honestly, and well.

And on the day when my file was burned in Syntagma Square – that day in 1977, when Greece was a riot of democracy – Maria was unable to attend. She, who was never denied. Who was now a professor: she was completing her first book. Typing, incessantly, her neck stiff, her shoulders hunched by her ears. Her body was gnarled by then. All except her breasts, which were already sagging. She never recovered her body after our children were born.

But now: back to when I was a child.

Story Number Three. Told by the waterfall, translated by your father: my words, his mouth, your body. Story Number Three.

I don't remember where he was, exactly. He was in the village, in a house that wasn't ours. My father couldn't come to our house: he was a targeted man. A wanted man. The whole Capitalist world wanted to capture my father, a rebel. A communist rebel. You know the history, yes? From all your books?

Anyway, the rebels were down from the mountains. They

needed food or weapons. Or maybe sex, I'm not sure. But he was there, in the village, in somebody's house, and I saw him. He was sleeping in bed; I sat on the floor and I watched him.

This is Story Number Three: my third memory.

Three of four: all I had.

He was a handsome man, Marianna. Broad face, Asiatic eyes. Stubby fingers, like mine. They were dirty: dirt in the crevices of his skin, absorbed inside the skin itself. But strong. He had strong hands. Muscle and girth, like mine. It is disturbing, the power these hands have: small, unmanly hands. Strong, but too small. But some women: What can I say? If I light their cigarette or offer a drink... if they see these fingers....

I don't understand it, Marianna.

You do: yes? You do?

This I did not reveal to your father: there was no need to hurt him.

Anyway, he had these hands. I know this because I watched him. For several hours, I watched my father lying in bed, asleep. Breathing.

I watched my father breathing.

His hands were on his belly.

And, Marianna, you must try to understand: every time I lie beside a woman, after, I imagine her watching me. I *feel* her watching me. It is palpable, this vision: my hands are limp on my chest; the hair is damp on my belly. I feel myself breathing. Marianna, I can almost *taste* myself. I can almost taste her desire to touch me.

And that is Story Number Three.

Drink it up, Marianna. Drink up the stories.

Deep and sloppy. Go ahead. Let them spill from the corners of your mouth. Just like that afternoon, before your father arrived: Easter with all our friends. Easter in a Greek mountain village. Romantic, yes? You were living the story. The myth of the modern Greeks: Kazantzakis' Greeks. Such sorrowful vitality: such tragic life in their bodies. So sensual, animal, smashing their plates in an erotic frenzy.

Yes? You thought you'd found home: your true Greek nature. Your blood, so vital. Your history: your story. Yes?

And I offered you drinks which you took from my hands. One, then another. You drank them sloppy.

Drink up the stories, Marianna.

You danced on the veranda while I watched. You danced, knowing I was watching. Drunk: we were all drunk that day. Dancing on our friend's veranda: that flat platform of irregular stones, the borders crawling with wild roses. Small roses: not your fat American roses. No, these flowers are small, their petals tight. Improbably soft on the vine beside the veranda. And beyond the roses: the slope toward the sea. That precipitous slope into the Aegean.

Do you remember?

No: I don't imagine that you do. I don't, because you can't actually *see* the water from the veranda: the Aegean itself is hidden. But if you'd looked, Marianna, you would've noticed: the light is different down there. The light over the water is eased. It is moist.

Maria looked. Maria saw. Even when she was young, Maria would've seen.

But you were too busy dancing with our friends: Dimitri, Stavros, Stavroula, Litsa. Beautiful friends and their beautiful children, just your age: Elena, Apostolus, Katarina... Elena, who fed you lamb. Who put her fingers in your mouth. Yes? All those bodies, dancing: women hissing on the ground; men leaping through the air; plates and glasses smashed to pieces. And you were in the middle, completely still. You and Elena. This stillness. Completely in focus, her fingers in your mouth.

I never dance, Marianna.

I like to watch.

But I do not dance: dancing is too obvious. Too crude. Besides, we weren't allowed to dance in the orphanage. But that is another story.

Story Number Four.

I almost forgot: Story Number Four. The fourth and final memory of my father. Given to you by the waterfall, the pit. And in this story, again, I do not see him. In this story, all I have is his voice.

I was young. It must've been 1941, right before my father joined the guerrillas. I was walking through the fields, picking grapes and eating some. They're not sweet, Marianna: you'd think they'd be sweet but they're not. They're astringent. And that is their taste: the way they suck the liquid from your mouth. Yes?

Anyway, I was eating grapes when I came to a group of men. They were working in the fields; my father was among them. I know, because I heard him say, 'Yiannouli, why don't you get us some water.'

'*Yiannouli,*' he said.

And I must explain: 'Yiannouli' is the diminutive form of my name. The endearing form. This is how my father called me in Story Number Four. Yiannouli.

And your father didn't translate that. There, by the water-fall, I didn't hear him say that sound: *Yiannouli*. He knew, like I knew: you wouldn't have understood. You, with all your questions and your 'needs': you wouldn't have grasped the subtlety of that moment.

Yiannouli. His voice.

Your father understood. Your kind, long-suffering father who answered all your questions, who told you his soul so you could write your book: he understood. And he kept this subtlety between him and me. *Yiannouli*. This we shared, we two Greek men: the son of a Communist and the son of a Conservative. A mutual epiphany. In that single moment, both of us realized: you wanted to make a story of us. You, this female creature, alluring us. Taking us to the waterfall. These two Greek men and you, in between, asking for our stories. Desiring some confrontation, some catharsis. The tension of it: your father, and you, and me. There by the waterfall, close to the pit: that pit we'd visited after Easter, before your father arrived. There. Just there.

Yes?

That's it: yes? The spot? Hm? Have I found the spot, Marianna? Am I touching too hard now: too direct?

You're not ready yet. I can feel this: your body isn't ready.

But I'll keep going, because this isn't mutual anymore.

You took our stories. You: so excited by our trauma. Our tragedy: these two Greek men.

Your excitement was vulgar.

And yet we let you, Marianna: you, beautiful female. Young, curious. You: we let you take our stories. Your father and I: our small memories, these tiny moments that swell to fill our selves. These moments that, when exposed to light, become naked and ugly. Shameful.

Yes: you pulled this from our bodies. We have all been sullied by this process.

Notes

Some names have been changed to protect the identities of the people involved in these stories. Some names have not been changed. Other names required no changing, because they do not refer to actual human beings.

The following stories first appeared, in different form, in various publications: "Layers" in *Slush Pile Magazine;* "What We Do for Money" in *Joyland;* and "You" in *Exile: The Literary Quarterly.*

A portion of "The Subject of the Game" was excerpted from The Lucky Child: A Novel (Mansfield Press, 2010).

The lines from Plato's "Laches" are taken from Iain Lane's translation, in Early Socratic Dialogues (Penguin, 1987), edited by Trevor J. Saunders.

The author wishes to acknowledge the support of the Ontario Arts Council and the Canada Council for the Arts.

Acknowledgements

I'd like to thank my family, especially my mother, Frances Apostolides. Although I matured as a writer through conversations with my father, I matured as a woman through conversations with my mom. I'd also like to thank my children, Athanasia and Romeo, whose love unfailingly brings me out of my head and into what is true.

Thanks, finally, to Jay MillAr, who gave me a literary home.

Colophon

Manufactured as the First Edition of
*Voluptuous Pleasure: The Truth About
the Writing Life* by BookThug in the
Spring of 2012. Distributed in Canada
by the Literary Press Group www.lpg.ca.
Distributed in the United States by Small
Press Distribution www.spdbooks.org.
Shop online at www.bookthug.ca

BOOK
PRODUCTION
WAR ECONOMY
STANDARD

Type + Design by Jay MillAr with
a thankful nod to Beautiful Outlaw